LOTTE'S LOCKET

by the same author

CURIOUS MISSIE

PLAIN GIRL

MIRACLES ON MAPLE HILL

Lotte's Locket

✹

VIRGINIA SORENSEN

Illustrated by Fermin Rocker

HARCOURT, BRACE & WORLD, INC., NEW YORK

The lyrics on pages 159 and 160 are from a series of propaganda songs written by Richard Dyer-Bennet for the Office of War Information in 1943 and are reprinted here with the kind permission of Mr. Dyer-Bennet.

Library of Congress Catalog Card Number: 64-17087
Printed in the United States of America
first edition

Odense, Denmark
April 2, 1964

Dearest Sue!

Well, here is that book at last! Did you think I'd never get it done? I did. Now it seems a lucky sign that I finish it on April 2, H. C. Andersen's birthday. And it seems a good day to write this letter and thank you for so patiently reading the manuscript last year.

Once you asked me whether a story was "true," and I told you, remember, that it was both true and untrue at the same time. So is this one about Lotte and her locket. It began with a true story about a real girl, but she was Norwegian, and it was her mother who had brought the old locket to America. I changed it all around, trying to make the real (and quite incredible) story seem more true! That's what storytellers have to do in this incredible world because even fairy stories seem simple now, don't you think? Anybody can fly. And yet the same old things go right on being wonderful, things like mothers and grandmothers and houses and animals and living light.

H. C. Andersen wrote a story once, imagining how it would be to fly. He called it "Thousands of Years from Now." Wouldn't he be surprised to know it has all happened in less than a hundred years? He wanted very much to come to America when he was invited but wrote to his friends here

47666

that he was afraid of the sea and always got sick at his stomach on a ship. He loved trains (because on his first journeys by stagecoach he got very sick) and of course he called them "Dragons."

I have been wishing today that you were here with me this spring. How many things we could see, the things Lotte sees. I can be a Danish Guidebook too!

And some day, in America, I want you to know my lovely Danish friend Hanne, after whom I named one of my heroines in another book. She has a little girl named Lotte! She married an American just as Mor did and came to live in Maine. Hanne Greaver is her name now (she was Nielsen in Denmark), and she has helped with this story more than I can say.

Let me know how you like Lotte. You were very nice not to mark many places red for "dull" on the manuscript, and I hope not many places will need marking now. But let me know, and we'll try to do better the next time.

Love,
Aunt Virginia

Contents

LOTTE'S LOCKET

CHAPTER ONE

❧

Patrick and a Lillegris

"Here they come," Lotte said.

She let the curtain fall over her window again so they wouldn't know she was watching. In case they noticed anything at all. Lately Mor didn't seem to notice anything or anybody but Patrick, Patrick, *Patrick*.

Lisa came and stood close behind to watch. Lotte felt her breath on the back of her neck. She moved a little to get away, but she didn't say a word. Lately she couldn't say anything much to Lisa about anything—but especially about Patrick. Lisa thought he was wonderful; she was just like the rest. Now she seemed pleased by the way Patrick and Mor were laughing as they got out of his big car. They were always laughing and going chatter-chatter-chatter. They went up the walk between Farmor's rosebushes. The front door opened and closed again after them. "In about ten minutes," Lotte said to Lisa then, "we can creep out and watch them having tea."

"Isn't it a *grand* car?" Lisa was still looking out of the window.

Lotte pulled her warm robe over her shoulders. "I think it's ugly," she said. "It's a big, old, nasty American Dollar-Grin, hogging all the roads."

She saw Lisa get her funny look. Lately everybody got funny looks. Yesterday even Farmor had said, "Lotte, Patrick is a wonderful man. And if your mother has found somebody she can love—it will be very good for her, don't you think? She's been lonely on the farm without any of her old friends."

Farmor didn't seem to think what it might *mean* if Mor— She couldn't even think about it. And Lisa, she was so silly she never thought what anything meant.

"Won't they get cross if you go out and watch them?" Lisa asked. "My Mor would fix me good if *I*—"

"They won't even know. I do it all the time and they never know. There's a nice place at the top of the stairs where I can see them and they can't see me."

Until now, except on great days like a birthday or Midsummer's Night, Mor had never let Lisa come and spend the whole night. But she didn't seem to care what anybody did any more. Except Patrick.

"Of course, we have to be quiet," Lotte said, and began to whisper as she turned the handle of the door. The first sound they heard in the hall was Mor laughing. She was laughing so hard at something Patrick said that Lotte knew she wouldn't hear anything. If the whole house fell down, she would go right on laughing at Patrick. She seemed to imagine that she was a young girl instead of a grown-up mother with a daughter going on eleven. She was laughing and talking and rushing around lately like a chicken with its head off.

As they moved along the hall, Lisa caught her foot in the edge of the rug and began to giggle.

"Ssssh!" Lotte turned and clapped a hand over Lisa's mouth. Lisa was apt to get the giggles at the wrongest times —in church or in assembly at school or in the middle of a hard test in arithmetic. "If they hear us, we'll be sent right back to bed!" They crept to the railing that curved around the top step and knelt together, peering down. The huge chandelier in the hall was burning right under them, and beyond that they could see through the glass doors that led from the hall into the sitting room. Farmor sat where she always did, at the coffee-table, behind her beautiful blue cups and saucers and her neat white napkins and a little row of shining that must be the spoons. There was a plate of cakes, frosted in different colors, and a plate of sandwiches, both brown and white. Nobody on earth could possibly eat as much as Patrick. He emptied all the dishes at the table every time he came and took sometimes three or four cakes at coffee. Farmor seemed to think it was wonderful, how much he ate, and Mor kept passing him things as if feeding him was the one thing she would rather do than anything in the whole world.

Lisa was breathing on her neck again, and she moved away. Sometimes lately she didn't like Lisa at all. Sometimes Lisa started getting on her nerves, especially when she giggled too much and talked about how wonderful Patrick was and rolled her eyes in a silly way and said, "Oh, love, love!"

How funny, Mor had taken off her shoes! Maybe her feet had got tired dancing. There she was, curled into her chair in stocking feet, as if Patrick wasn't even company any more. Of course he never looked like company. He never really looked dressed up but just loungy and big in his sporty American clothes. Sometimes he didn't even wear a tie at lunch but had his shirt open over the hair on his chest. Mor had always hated sloppy people, but she didn't seem to mind anything Patrick did.

Farmor was pouring tea from her best pot, the one she called the Blue Duchess. Mor kept picking up the plate and passing it to Patrick as if he couldn't help himself.

"It makes me hungry to watch," Lisa whispered into her ear.

"We'll go down and get something as soon as they go to bed," Lotte whispered back.

Just then the hall door opened, and there was Finn, the nice plump man who took care of all Farmor's animals. He looked in a hurry, and the minute he knocked at the sitting room door Farmor jumped up.

"Sorry to bother you, but you wanted to know—" Finn held his hat steady in his hand, as if something—ya, something *was* in it. "The sow is doing fine, but this one was a runt, one of the littlest I ever saw. I thought we'd better keep him in for a day or so." Farmor was looking into his hat, and she reached in—

"Oh, *look!*" Lisa whispered, and Lotte breathed deeply. Farmor was holding the tiniest pink thing you ever saw.

"A real runt," Finn said.

"I'll carry him out and fix the box," Farmor said. "Does he need a bottle tonight?"

Lotte couldn't hear Finn's answer; they disappeared into the back hall, and the door closed after them. And right

away, as if all they had waited for was to be alone, Patrick
and Mor began to kiss.

"Look, they're—" Lisa whispered, forgetting all about the
little pig.

"Ssssh!" Lotte hissed at her. But they wouldn't have heard
anything, she knew that. It had happened before, just a few
nights ago; and she could have fallen downstairs head over
heels without their hearing. "Maybe," she whispered now,
"Farmor will let me have that *lillegris* for a pet. Once
before there was a runt, and I gave him his bottle all the
time."

The hall felt cold now; a draft had come in when Finn
opened the door. Through the door of the sitting room,
Lotte could see the soft lamplight and the dancing of the
fire in the grate. It was cozy in there at night, drinking tea
and eating cake and sandwiches. And kissing. "When Patrick goes home," she whispered, "we'll go down and eat
by the fire and look at the *lillegris*—shall we?"

"Wouldn't your Farmor care?"

"She won't know. She'll be in bed."

Lisa giggled. *"Fun!"* she said.

The door opened again, and Farmor came back to her tea.
Patrick went to the fire and put on some more sticks, as he
often did lately. He was always saying how much he liked
an open fire and how he wished he had one in his apartment
in New York City. When Lotte asked him how he kept
warm, he said the problem in America was to keep a house
cool enough in wintertime, even though he lived so high
in the air he could look down on the birds.

Who would want to look *down* at birds? "Even skylarks?"
Lotte had asked, and he laughed and said New York had
no skylarks, only skyscrapers.

Well, now, Lotte thought, at last he was going. Just four
more days and he would be gone.

Lisa whispered, "I'm cold. I'm going back to bed."

"I'll come in a minute." Lotte wanted to watch until
Patrick left. One night Mor came out into the hall with
him and held his coat, and he grabbed her and you would
have thought he would break her ribs like the man in one
of the songs he sang with his big guitar. Afterward, Mor
had sat down there with Farmor talking and talking, and
Lotte thought they'd never come to bed. Mor always came
in to see her and tuck the covers around. But that night she
hadn't come. How many nights ago? Two. . . . It seemed
a long time ago already with so much to worry about.

She heard the door close after Lisa and almost wished
she had gone too. She was shivering all over. When Farmor
poured more tea, a nice little smoke of steam came off the
cup. They were warm and cozy down there together.

Suddenly Patrick stood up, and Mor too, and they came
out into the hall together. But he wasn't going for his coat.
Oh, dear, they were starting for the stairs! She stood up
quickly, thinking she would run for her room.

"Why, Lotte, what on earth are you doing up?"

Patrick laughed. "So—we have a Peeping Lotte!" he said.

"Couldn't you sleep?" Mor asked anxiously. "Why didn't
you come down where it's warm?" She rushed over and
put her arms around Lotte, and then, suddenly, something

terrible happened in Lotte's throat. She got such a lump she couldn't say a word.

"Have you caught cold? Pat, she's freezing. I think she has a fever—"

Now, how terrible and stupid, Lotte began to cry. Mor said, "Darling—" and "You're absolutely freezing!" and sure enough Lotte was shivering all over. "Pat, carry her down by the fire."

Lotte was lifted into his huge arms. "No—*no*—" But it was no use to struggle, he was already carrying her down the stairs. Farmor hurried to the door; what a lovely fuss they all made! Hot milk was sent for, and she was wrapped in a rug from the couch, and then she too sat there by the fire with a steaming cup.

"I just came out to watch you having tea. Lisa and I both came out—she wanted to see—but she got cold. I saw Finn bring in that little runt. Farmor—could—"

"Of course, Finn will fetch him in," Farmor said.

And in two minutes he was on Lotte's lap, and she was holding the nipple of a bottle in his mouth. Finn had a very gentle voice for so big a man. "There was no room for this little one at the big table," he said. Lotte knew what he meant; she had seen other runts out in the pens and knew how they got trampled and pushed out of the way while their big brothers and sisters grabbed every single teat the mother had. Once Finn had told her about a sow who was so bothered by the trouble a poor little runt caused that she decided to eat him up. How awful! She looked down at the tiny creature on her lap and touched him with her fingertips. Such a softness. He seemed to be asleep, but the minute he felt her fingers he turned and searched for them to suck. There—he caught at one.

Lotte looked up. "Can't he be my pet, Farmor?" His nose was as soft as a kitten's. It was like a small pink button. He was a million times nicer than a doll and at least four times as sweet as a kitten. He looked darling and comical at the same time, with one little hoof hanging over the towel Finn had wrapped around him, his eyes fast shut and his ears like tiny quivering shells. He had long pale eyelashes. "I'll call him Lotte's Lillegris."

They were all smiling. Finn said, "He'll make a good pet until Ida has something to say about that box in her kitchen."

"I'll take care of him," Lotte said. "We'll make him a special little pen."

"*Ja—ja,*" Finn said.

"But you could hardly take him to America," Farmor said.

There was a sudden silence in the room. Lotte felt her heart beating hard and slow.

At last, Mor said, "Pat and I were going to tell you the first thing in the morning, Lotte. We—" Her face was pink, and her eyes shining, and she came over and leaned down for a kiss. "Pat and I are going to be married. Very soon. And all of us are going to America on a big ship."

Farmor's face was just as pink, just as smiling. And Patrick had the biggest smile of all, of course; he always had the biggest of everything. Lotte's face was as red as a Christmas cabbage. When he came over to her and took a kiss, she went stiff all over, and her heart was beating so hard she could feel it to her fingertips. She leaned down and laid her cheek against the soft nose of Lillegris, who gave a funny grunt and wiggled against her and searched for her finger.

"What do you say?" Mor looked anxious and lifted Lotte's face, a finger under her chin.

"Of course Lotte is going to be happy if you are," Farmor said. "It takes getting used to. Lotte—imagine, America! I've always wanted to go to America."

"And now you'll be coming very soon," Patrick said. "Why don't all of us go together?"

Mor said, "What a lovely idea!"

But Farmor shook her head. *"I'm* not going along on a honeymoon. I'll come next year."

"I thought—" Lotte began but could not say it, for the lump was once more in her throat. In four days Patrick had been planning to fly away.

"You thought I was going this week, didn't you?" Patrick had a way of knowing what people were thinking. His voice was joking and light, and he sat down beside her. "I was going, Lotte, but I found out I couldn't leave your mother. I never want to leave her again—" and his voice changed in an odd way. "Never as long as I live." He looked at Mor, and Mor looked at him, and it was as if Lotte and Farmor had gone away and left them alone. "And since your mother doesn't like to fly, we're going by sea. I've been able to postpone going home for two more weeks so we can have a little wedding. By then you can all be ready to go with us. Don't you think?"

She could not speak.

"I'm glad we could tell you tonight," Mor said. "We didn't dream you were still awake. And we did want to tell you together."

Silence again. Lotte looked at the fire and Lillegris and
rubbed around his little ears. Then Farmor said briskly,
"And now Lillegris and Lotte must get to bed."

Finn lifted Lillegris from Lotte's lap and carried him
away. And Mor said, "Sleepy girl—" and Patrick said, "I'll
carry her up," and Lotte felt his big arms come around her
again.

"No," she said suddenly, "I'm not sleepy at all. I can walk
by myself."

"Okay." Patrick set her on her feet, and Lotte could feel
Mor's eyes meet his over her head. "See you in the morning."

When Mor and Lotte got to the top of the stairs, Mor
whispered, "Let's not wake Lisa," and she opened the door
very softly. While she tucked in the covers and fluffed Lotte's
pillow around her ears, she said in a low voice, "When we
found you, Pat and I were on the way to the Lotte Room.
He's never seen it, and Farmor was telling him about it
tonight. We promised you'd tell him the Lotte story tomorrow."

Lotte did not answer, and Mor sat down in the chair by
the bed. Every night, until lately, she had sat in the Reading
Chair; Lotte had fallen asleep hundreds of times as she
listened to stories from her favorite books.

"Lotte, I hope you're not going to be too upset," Mor said.
Lotte closed her eyes tight.

"Patrick loves you very much. He wants to do all the things
for you that your own Far would have done. He loved your
Far—that's what seems so wonderful. It's a miracle really—
to think he came to Denmark to visit, not even *knowing*—"

Lotte did not need to be reminded. She remembered very

well the day Patrick had appeared at the door and asked for Far. They had been fliers together during the war, he said.

"It's not that I think he will take Far's place. Not for me, either, you know that, Lotte. But it's true, as Farmor says, you need more than two women. And I—" Lotte only wished she would stop now, say good night, and go away. "He's wonderful, Lotte, so kind and good, and he understands just how you feel. So do I, and so does Farmor. But we all think you'll have a happy time going to America and meeting lots of new friends—" She glanced toward the bed where Lisa lay, breathing deeply.

I don't want any new friends, Lotte thought. I just want Lisa. But she only lay still as if she had fallen alseep. She did not want to go away from Lottegaard, either, or Farmor or Finn or Ida or all the people she knew—or Lille-gris—or Denmark—

"Tomorrow everything will seem better," Mor said gently. Lotte could hear the chair making its familiar little squeak as it rocked gently back and forth. She kept her eyes closed and pretended to breathe deeply, as Lisa did, and after a time Mor stood up and went softly out. Lotte heard her going down the stairs and heard their voices, far off, and Patrick's big laugh.

America. Farmor too! If the idea of Farmor's leaving Lottegaard and Denmark did not make you cry, it would make you laugh. Why, Farmor had lived here since the minute she was born, and her mother too, and *her* mother, and *her* mother— Seven Lottes in a row had lived at Lottegaard. "Now eight, with you," Farmor often said.

All I will have to do, Lotte thought, staring up into the dark, is tell Mor that I won't leave Denmark or Lottegaard, ever, not as long as I live. Mor would not leave her here alone, she knew, not for Patrick or anybody. All she had to do was make it perfectly plain, and then Patrick would fly off by himself . . .

At last she heard the Dollar-Grin go roaring down the road. And then she heard Farmor and Mor coming upstairs together. The hall lights stopped shining under the door. *Now*— She crept over to Lisa's bed and touched her lightly. "Lisa—" Whispering, not to scare her. *"Lisa."* And Lisa sat up.

"They've all gone to bed now. Let's go down."

Once more they slipped out of the door. A small lamp burned in the hall as always. "They caught me out here, and I went down," she whispered. "Lillegris is in the kitchen."

When they opened the door to the dining room, it looked strange in the tiny stream of light from the hall. Ida had set the table for breakfast, and the silver and dishes gave little glints of light; and now they saw that a fire was still burning in the kitchen stove and shone softly through the front of the firebox. And there—*ja, ja,* there was Lillegris, in a little box behind the stove, lying on clean straw and a folded towel.

They knelt on either side.

"He's so soft—like a baby—"

"He *is* a baby."

He had seemed to be asleep, but the minute he felt a finger he turned and seized it. "Let him suck mine too," Lisa said, and they both began to laugh.

"Ssssh, they'll hear us."

"Let's see if we can find some milk. Finn had a bottle." Lotte found it, half full of milk, on the other side of the stove, keeping warm. Lillegris seized it at once, and they knelt on either side, watching him. "They always think you're going to feed them when you touch them," Lotte said. "Baby birds are the same, aren't they? When I go into the *svinehus,* every one of those pigs, big ones and all, start grunting and butting the walls."

"Animals don't know anything but just to eat and sleep," Lisa said, stroking Lillegris tenderly. "I'd rather hold a baby pig than a doll, wouldn't you?"

"His ears are like little shells."

"Look at his tiny hoofs—how *pink!*"

He had enough milk already. His head was tucked on his tiny hoofs, and he was sound asleep. "I'm going to make a special pen and have Lillegris for my special pet," Lotte said. "Maybe I can teach him some tricks. I heard of one, once—"

"That was in a story. It wasn't true," Lisa said.

"But he's smart. You can tell how smart he is by the way he knows how to eat from a bottle already. He was born just a few hours ago. That's a lot to know already." She sat back on her heels, looking at the sleeping baby. If Mor went off to America—of course she wouldn't, only if she *did*—I could take Lillegris and go off and join a carnival, she thought. Mor would read in a newspaper about LOTTE OF LOTTEGAARD AND HER WONDERFUL LILLEGRIS. It would be better than the flea circus at Tivoli. It would be lots better than a performing dog, because lots of dogs were clever. And everybody in Denmark especially loved pigs. Weren't they known as the "Wealth of Denmark"? That's what an article in *Politiken* said.

"Look at him wrinkling his nose—"

"He's having a dream."

Suddenly Lisa said, "When you go to America, I'll take care of him."

Lotte felt as if somebody had opened the door of the stove in her face. Even her eyes burned. When she spoke her voice trembled. "How did you know I might go to America? Were you awake when we came upstairs—I thought you were asleep—"

"No, I heard it yesterday. All the kids were talking about it."

Well, even before she had known for sure herself.

"It's not true! I'm *not* going to America—and neither is Mor. And neither is Farmor."

Lisa's face was even redder than Lotte's. "I only thought— I'm sorry, Lotte! I thought it was wonderful. I was going to tell you how glad I was."

"You're *glad?*" Lotte jumped up, her fists clenched, and Lisa stared up at her, surprised. Even Lillegris stirred uneasily in his sleep.

"Lotte, I—"

Lotte turned and walked with dignity out of the room and through the dining room and the hall and up the stairs. She did not even speak to Lisa, who followed meekly behind her.

"Lotte—"

But Lotte got into her bed and pulled the feather quilt up to her chin. "Turn off the lamp as soon as you're in," she said in a stiff, cold voice.

Presently, out of the dark, Lisa said, "Lotte, I only thought it was grand for your Mor. It's sad, her without any husband or any house of her own or any babies or *any*thing. Everybody thinks so."

Lotte stared at her in the darkness.

And then Lisa said a thing that made her blush a little. "And he's so nice and *rich.* You know how Americans are— and especially the ones from Texas. Far says he has an oil well all his own. And he flies a little airplane—he told Far about that! And he goes to Arabia and places in jets."

Lotte seemed not to hear any of these marvels but only tied herself into the tightest possible knot under the feather quilt.

"Your Mor's been lonesome without any Far around. Everybody knows that." Lisa went on. "Remember how lonesome we always said Tove was and all the women whose husbands died in the war?" Lotte did remember, but she did not say so. She only made herself tighter and tighter until she was like the kernel of a nut.

"Tove says it's bad for girls to grow up without any Far. Or any Farfar either. Lots of the women have gotten married again."

Still Lotte did not speak or move.

"And Patrick is so nice and funny." When he first came, they had agreed about this. Once, because Lotte was so tall and Lisa so short, Patrick had given them new names in English. "You're a Lot o' Lotte," he had said, "and Lisa is a lot less. So I think I'll call you Lotta and Lessa."

They had rolled on the floor laughing, and had called each other Lotta and Lessa for a long time, until Lotte decided Patrick was not nearly so funny as she had thought. Now she ached all over from being so tight and thought, *If only Lisa would shut up!* Sometimes, lately, she had stopped liking Lisa for as much as a whole day!

"Lotte, are you asleep?"

No answer. And at last Lisa too lay still.

When they went up to the Lotte Room, Lotte thought, that would be the best time to say how she felt. It would be easy for Mor to see, up there, how important Lottegaard was and how nobody could ever leave it. Mor was not a Lotte; of course, that made a difference. But she had always understood everything before Patrick came. It had been Mor who told her about the Lottes, so long ago she couldn't remember the first time. Maybe in Copenhagen, before they came here to live with Farmor, in that same chair, sitting by the same bed. "And they lived at Lottegaard, every one of them . . ." One Lotte after the other. Sometimes, when they went to the Lotte Room, there was a funny feeling as if all of the Lottes, smiling down from their portraits, every one in the same dress, were all alive and might suddenly begin to speak. It made her shiver sometimes, thinking about them in the night. When the house creaked and the wind blew the shutters and the curtains flapped—it was strange to think of all those Lottes walking around this very house, taking care of the floors and the beds and the food, carrying around the huge bunch of keys Farmor said they kept by them all the time. "And someday I will give these very keys to you," Farmor had said. "And when you are confirmed, I will hang the locket around your neck."

Lotte's locket.

Certainly Mor knew that Lotte's locket could never, never, never be taken to America—thousands of miles away, where people did not even speak Danish, where people like Patrick thought Denmark was no bigger than a pin, no bigger than one of the tiniest states in America. Patrick said one day that Denmark would fit into such a little corner of Texas that if it blew away some night, nobody would notice. She hated him when he said things like that. Even Farmor, though, was apt to say, "Of course, Denmark is very small— and our money is little too."

But other people, like Hr. Axel— When he came here on the Fifth of May to help celebrate the heroes, he said there was a marvelous thing about Denmark—*"The farther you look back the bigger she is."*

Patrick had heard it, too. And he had read the fine things Hr. Axel wrote in his newspaper about the brave things the men in this neighborhood did "under the war." And Patrick had said in his ugly old English, "You mean *during* the war?" And Hr. Axel said, *"Ja, ja, during* the war. My English is not so good," and he had blushed to make such a mistake. But of course he made no mistakes when he wrote his newspaper pieces in good *Dansk!* And Patrick didn't know any Danish except a few things like "thanks" and "hello" and "good-by" and "mister," which was written "Hr.," and he pronounced them all wrong, every time, and said he had read in a book that Danish was "like a disease of the throat."

Why couldn't Mor have fallen in love with Hr. Axel instead of with Patrick? Lotte had prayed and prayed that Mor would fall in love with Hr. Axel, for Hr. Axel was certainly in love with her. You could tell. And year after year he came here to help celebrate Peace Day, and once he made a speech and marched with the widows and orphans to the monument and helped put flowers there. And twice he had helped light candles in the windows of Lottegaard. The last time, before Patrick came, Lotte felt how much he was in love with Mor. It would be fun to live in Copenhagen again and to come to Lottegaard every summer as she had done before. In only one night, on the boat from Copenhagen, one could come to Aalborg and then on a little red train—the little lightning train, people called it—almost to the farm.

Once Hr. Axel said, "What a beautiful woman your mother is!" And of course, it was true. Everybody was in

love with Mor, who was sweet and lovely and had a voice
like a bird and could dance like a fairy and who dressed
sometimes for the opera or the ballet in shoes like Cinderella's and had a long white cloak edged with fur almost as
lovely as any of the Lotte clothes in the big oak chest.

"Please," she whispered into the dark, and tears squeezed
out and began to run down into the pillow. "Please let Mor
love Hr. Axel instead of Patrick." She was not mean enough
to want Mor to go on being lonely, to have to live here
in the country all the time where they could not go to the
National Museum and to art museums like the wonderful
new one and to all the grand Copenhagen things like pro-
cessions when famous people and kings and queens came
to visit. Here, Mor sighed when she read about these things
in the newspaper. She loved Copenhagen. It was her city,
where she grew up. "You mustn't stay here and bury yourself," Farmor had said in the beginning. But Mor said, "I
can't be alone in Copenhagen any more." It made her sad
to go to places she had gone with Far, to wear the clothes
he had loved, and to do the things they had loved to do together. Gradually she had seemed to become happy again.
And then—Patrick.

She snuggled deep under the *dyne,* comforted by the softness of the feathers. One thing Patrick said was true: a Danish bed is like a nest. In America, he said, there were fluffy
blankets, but hardly eight inches thick. "I have an *electric*
blanket," he had said, and Lisa's mouth had fallen open
with silly wonder. "It's full of nice little wires—"

She had stopped crying. She tried to make some more

tears, thinking how miserable she was, but it was hard to make tears when nobody was around to see or care.

The wind sighed around the chimneys. No wonder Danes had made themselves nests in this land of wind. She remembered H. C. Andersen's story of Valdemar Daae and his daughters, and what the wind had said to them. It could tell all the things that had happened since time began, for, of course, the wind could go anywhere and could see and hear everything. Once there had been such a strong wind that it blew the thatch off one side of the house and the stork's wheel up by the chimney had been found, the next day, far down the road.

CHAPTER TWO

The Story of Lotte's Locket

When Lisa and Lotte came down to breakfast, Patrick was there already. Mor and Farmor were feeding him again.

"I know it's shocking to Danes," Patrick said, "but sometimes in New York I actually have to eat an egg that is *more than one day old.*"

"How awful!" Farmor said.

"But it's a good thing I'm going back where the food doesn't come so fresh and so often," Patrick said. "I've gotten so fat here I've had to move every last button on my clothes."

Mor looked as if she thought this was wonderful, passing him the butter which Farmor always arranged in little designs on the plate.

"*Tooth*butter!" Patrick said. "Tove told me the first day at the inn that the reason she put so much butter on my *smørrebrød* was that every good Dane liked it thick enough to show the shape of all his teeth."

"That is so," Mor said.

"She was planning our *fest* this morning when I came down," Patrick said. "You and I, Gerda, are supposed to come over and tell her everything we want. The menu she suggested! From soup to nuts—the *works!*"

"Maybe we shouldn't have it so elaborate," Mor said, looking at Farmor.

"Why not? A wedding is a big celebration," Farmor said. "Either we have a simple ceremony here at home or we go to the inn and everybody in the neighborhood must come."

Lisa reached out and pressed Lotte's hand, excited. A wedding at the *kro!*

"Lisa," Farmor said, "your mother telephoned. And I told her I thought you might like to stay and go with us to see the things in the Lotte Room. I'm going to take everything out of the chest today."

For Patrick, Lotte thought, and felt the bread she was eating dry in her throat. But no matter how miserable she might feel, it was fun to go up the stairs and see the old room where she felt so special. Lisa always said she wished *she* had been born something like a Lotte of Lottegaard. It was a little bit like being a princess. To be a princess you had to be born to somebody else who was a princess; and to be a Lotte you had to be born into a long line of Lottes.

"When Lotte is confirmed," Farmor was saying as they went up the stairs, "she will wear the old wedding dress and the locket and have her portrait painted. Maybe all this fuss seems foolish nowadays—some people think it is—but somehow I don't want to be the one to stop it. *Eight* Lottes!"

"Sometimes," Patrick said very seriously, "I wish we had places in Texas where we belonged the way you belong here. My great-grandfather came from a farm in Ireland, and every one of my folks has lived in a different place. Not to speak of me. I had lived in four different places before I was ten years old."

Ida had opened the shutters of the Lotte Room, and it was flooded with sunshine. There was a fire burning in the tall tile stove, too, so that the old room seemed alive and you might almost think somebody had slept there the night before. The huge, high bed with its posters almost to the ceiling and its gold silk curtains and coverlet stood as always, though, undisturbed.

On the walls hung portraits of all the Lottes, smiling down. The last one was of Farmor when she was a young girl with blue eyes that looked directly into yours and seemed to turn and follow you around the room. The first Lotte was the most beautiful of all, even though she looked quite fat. She had her hair in a cluster of golden curls on top of her head and hanging down over her ears. Every Lotte wore the same locket, and it was at this, in painting after painting, that Patrick looked. "That locket is what I'm eager to see," he said.

"Imagine," Farmor said, drawing Lotte to her side. "I was the first Lotte in two hundred years not to produce a daughter! Everyone said the whole thing had come to an end with me. And then my son married, and along came another one. I had almost decided to do as Hr. Axel said and give everything to a museum where it could be taken care of properly."

"Farmor! How *awful!*" Lotte said. The idea of the Lotte things in a museum gave her a chill. In museums were all those old beds that nobody ever slept in, chairs nobody ever sat in, stoves that never had any fires. And chests with nothing at all inside—locked. She couldn't say another word, it seemed so terrible.

Lisa stood absolutely still, looking solemn. "That," Lotte

said to her, pointing up at the first Lotte, "is my great-great-great-great-great-*great* grandmother. She lived when Frederik V was King of Denmark." She had learned to bring people up to the Lotte Room and tell them these things. There had been eight kings since then, four Christians and four Frederiks. Eight kings take a long, long time.

"In some ways," Farmor was saying, "my confirmation day seemed more important than my wedding day, because I wore the locket for the first time. What a *fest* we had! My mother wrote a long poem about my childhood and about the Lottes, and my father made up the words to a song, and everybody made speeches, and afterward I took six big wreaths and put one on the grave of each Lotte. What a day!" She stood looking at the chest, in her hands an iron key six inches long. "This chest has been here longer than any of the Lottes, as you can see," she said. On the front of the huge oak chest, which was bound with wide iron bands, was the date *1684.*

Patrick leaned down and traced a finger along the edge of the lock, which was very fancy, with lots of bolts in designs. Lotte could not remember when she first saw the chest. It was when she was a very little girl and the whole family had come up to get out the christening clothes. Mor had told her about it. "And your father set you down into the chest, just for fun," she said. "You looked like a doll. And you yelled to get out." Another time Lotte remembered very well. That was the time when she and Mor came up to put away Far's things, his watch and his medals and some of the clothes he wore that Mor wanted to keep. "Someday you will want these," she had said. Sometimes Lotte wished she could not remember that sad time. But she kept remembering it whether she wanted to or not.

"Will you open it, Patrick?" Farmor asked. "It gets harder every year."

It seemed all wrong for Patrick to be the one to turn the big key and lift the heavy lid. But he was serious enough. Lotte rather wished he would say something dumb in his loud Texas voice, just to show Mor he didn't belong here at all. But he didn't. He didn't say a word, only stood looking down. A smell of old dried rose-petals came into the room, and another smell, which must be age, no more than a dusty catch in the throat.

Ida spread a sheet on the floor, as always, so Farmor could lay out the precious things. Every spring, during house-cleaning, Farmor opened the chest and took everything out, shaking the dresses and the petticoats and bonnets and shawls and things that belonged to the Lottes. There was an embroidered waistcoat so tiny that it barely fitted around Lotte's waist, and a satin purse on a long ribbon. There were shoes almost like the ones that ballerinas wore, made of white satin and tied with ribbons. And the wedding dress itself. Once when Hr. Axel came, Farmor had taken all the tissue paper away and had laid it on the high bed, tumbling with old rose leaves. And a white veil and a tiny lace cap. And of course the locket. "There, you can imagine how beautiful she looked," she had said, and they decided to take a photograph then, and Hr. Axel called his newspaper, and Farmor put it all on, and a man came and took pictures, and one Sunday there it was in print. Now there was a page in Farmor's House Book where the picture and story were pasted and covered with a plastic sheet to keep it nice.

"I imagine you've heard the Lotte story, Patrick," Farmor said. "But I think it would be nice if Lotte told it to you here. Don't you?"

"I hoped for that," he said. "I'd like to hear it from Lotte the Eighth, and right here, in the very room."

"Let me get the locket first," Farmor said. In one end of the big chest a tiny chest had been built; it had a secret sliding board at the bottom so that underneath precious things could be safely kept. If you hadn't been told, you wouldn't dream the secret place was there. "This was the safety-deposit box in the old time," Farmor said.

There it was, the locket, in its faded blue velvet box.

How beautiful it was! Lotte could hear Lisa breathing beside her as they all stood looking. It was made of shining yellow gold, and carved on it, with sprays of leaves and flowers and birds, were the letters L—O—T—T—E. The leaves were tiny emeralds, and the flowers were diamonds and rubies and rose topaz. One of the birds had a garnet eye. Farmor pushed the tiny catch, and the locket flew open. Inside was a tiny portrait of the first Lotte and her white-haired husband in their wedding clothes. It was done so delicately that one could not imagine how the painter could have found brushes fine enough.

Lotte had seen it many times, but her excitement was always the same. One day, when she was confirmed, Farmor would bring her here and take the locket out and hang it around her neck. What a moment that would be!

Farmor stood looking down at it, now, in silence, and then she handed it to Patrick so that he could study the design.

"Beautiful!" He spoke more softly than Lotte had dreamed he could.

"We all wore it to be married, just as the first Lotte did," Farmor said, and beside Patrick's voice hers sounded very matter-of-fact. "Confirmation, marriage, every great family festival. I think nowadays, there isn't enough thinking about old things for festivals. The world is changing, yes, and people move about; they don't stay in their old homes any more. And yet—" She smiled. "I think the old stories should be remembered and told to the children."

Patrick was nodding seriously, and Lotte saw him look at Mor. "I would like to have some old things to tell my children about," he said. "If I ever have any children." And then he looked at Lotte. "Now, at least, I will have a daughter," he said, and it was as if he had only now thought of this. He looked at the locket again and then again at Lotte and said in a kind of wonder, "Imagine—a daughter!"

"And she will bring plenty of old things with her," Mor said, and laughed, and the air became light again. "Lotte, would you like to tell the story now?"

Suddenly Lotte felt stubborn. Let Mor know that she didn't want to tell Patrick their old family story, not right here in the Lotte Room by the Lotte chest with all of the portraits looking down and seeming to listen. He didn't belong here, not at all.

"I'd rather not tell it today," she said.

There was an odd silence. And then Mor said, "Well, then, Farmor—"

"I guess Lotte is getting tired of that old story," Farmor said. "Last summer we must have had a hundred groups of people—it was because of that piece in the paper—"

They all sat down, Lisa and Lotte on the floor by the piled-up things. "People go to the inn, and then they come over here," Farmor said. "I tell Tove that if it keeps up, we will serve tea here and make our fortune. Sometimes I wonder how the story has changed with all the telling; I find myself adding little things—and I know Lotte does."

As she began to tell the story, she laid the locket down on her lap. Sitting in an old chair in the old room under the row of portraits, she looked very beautiful, Lotte thought. Her hair was white now, not gold as it was in her portrait, but her eyes were as blue as ever.

"The first Lotte was the daughter of a farmer who lived near Randers," she said. "Her father had been prosperous at one time, but there had been very hard times, and when Lotte was born, the family was faced with the possibility of losing their house and the old farm on which they had always lived. When this little girl was born, her father looked at her and said, 'Well, this one will make our fortune!' There was a story about a king who fell in love with a country girl and took her to Copenhagen and built her a castle and made her his queen. And anyway, people believed in fairies in those days, and in almost every fairy story there was a beautiful young girl for a prince to fall in love with! Anyway, the story goes that Jørgen Knudsen, Lotte's father, told everybody, all her life, that this beautiful girl was destined for marvelous things. But what did she do? When she was fifteen, she fell in love with a boy on the next farm. His name was Anders Carlsen, and Lotte Jørgensdatter wanted nothing on earth but to marry her nice young man and live on a little farm with him. But he was a youngest son and belonged to a big family. He hadn't a prospect in the world. So Lotte's parents refused to let him come to the house.

"Lotte had rather a temper, they say. She was terribly angry at her parents for refusing her lover and accused them of caring more for land and money than they did for their own daughter's happiness. One night, young Anders came secretly, and she planned to meet him and run away. But her father found out and set the dogs on him. It seems that people were very rough in those old days!"

Lotte had begun to wish she were telling the story, but of course it was too late now. She knew how to make the part about the dogs very exciting.

Lisa's eyes were as round as *kroner*. You would think she had never heard the story before when, as a matter of fact, Lotte had told it to her dozens of times. They had even played it all out, with costumes, at school. Once they had played it out for a family *fest* at Hyggehuset on the Fifth of May. It was their favorite acting-piece except the Underground. Of course, it was better here in this very room than anywhere else.

"Poor young Anders was told that if he ever came near the place again, he would be beaten, that Lotte was not for him. He was told that she was going to marry a very rich man, which at that time was only her parents' hope. Or so we think. It might be that they had made arrangements— who knows? At any rate, he tried and tried to see her, but one day a war broke out—there is always a war—and off he went.

" 'If he dies, I will kill myself!' That's what people say poor Lotte said. She had a good deal of spirit. You can see that in her portrait, don't you think? But soon word came that he had fallen in love with another girl and had married her in Copenhagen. Poor Lotte! She could not believe it at first, but his very brothers and sisters said it was true. Then how she scolded her father and mother for what they had done! And she stamped her foot and said, 'Now I will marry the first free man who comes into that door—you will see! No matter who he is, I will marry him. You have cared nothing for my happiness; now I will care nothing for yours!'

"And she sat down and waited for the door to open.

"They were terrified. A hired man, any poor old neighbor, might come in. Who could tell? She would not let them go out of the room. And there they sat, waiting. At last a knock came on the door. Lotte stood up and flung it open."

This was the part Lotte loved best, next to the ending.

"There stood a very old man, a white-haired neighbor who was very, very rich. When Lotte's father saw him, he stood up and rushed forward to shake his hand. The old man was a widower, and nobody knew how much gold he had, but horses and carriages and land and fine furniture and a splendid old farmhouse—all this they had seen. He seemed very pleased that he would get such a pretty young bride. He had been leading a very dreary life since his wife had died, and he had no children to comfort him.

"Nothing could have pleased Lotte's parents more. And since she always did as she said she would do, she carried out her promise. Then they say the old man's life became very lively again! She came to his house—this very one we live in—and changed everything. She bought herself beautiful new clothes and had fine new furniture made. She had many people come to her house and gave balls and parties and invited artists to sing and play for her guests. At the other end of the house—you have seen it—is the big room where she had her balls. Now we are keeping bags of grain there! It is too large entirely."

Once more Farmor looked down at the locket. "This was her wedding gift. The old man ordered it made by a very great jeweler in Copenhagen, one who had made jewelry for the King, they say. He could not do enough for his young bride; he was anxious that she should be happy. And she made him a very fine wife. She was a good manager and a good cook who could teach her servants to make everything properly. And she grew to love her kind husband very much. A few years after her marriage, her sweetheart came back home again. It was not true about his marriage; somebody had made it up; who was so cruel nobody knows. Perhaps Lotte's own parents started the rumor, though one doesn't like to think so. Anyhow he came, and he had been in the army all that time and had saved a good deal of money; he had become an officer. He came to see Lotte in his splendid uniform and asked her to leave her husband and run off with him to Copenhagen. But she refused. She had made a promise, she said, and now she would keep it.

"Everybody agrees she was a very great lady and a very fine wife. Everywhere her old husband went, she went with him. As he grew older, she took care of him and of his property. When he lay dying at last, he insisted that the name of the farm must be changed to Lottegaard, after her. It had borne the name of his first wife before, the woman for whom he had built it in the beginning. And when he died—" Farmor paused. Lotte understood why.

When she herself told the story, she always paused at that same place. The story had to be stopped while you felt sorry for the kind old man.

"He left a letter." Farmor drew the letter from the same secret place where the locket was kept. "All of the important papers of the house were kept here," she said, and touched the dark red seal, dried and broken. "This is his farewell letter and his will. It is so faded now that I keep it in this little case. Hr. Axel had copies made so the letter could be read without having to touch the old one at all— but I know it by heart, anyhow. *'To my good wife Lotte of Lottegaard,* I leave all of my goods and my land and my house. It is my hope that she marry and bear children, for she is yet young. If she should bear a daughter, let it have her name and inherit the house, even though there should be sons. The locket with her name upon it shall forever be the seal of her inheritance. And if there be a generation without a daughter, then the first daughter of the eldest son shall inherit Lottegaard and the locket which is the seal, and her name also shall be Lotte.' "

Always, when the story came to these words, Lotte felt a deep thrill of excitement and happiness. *Lotte of Lottegaard.*

"I was the first Lotte not to have a daughter," Farmor said. "How guilty I felt! Like a queen who cannot bear an heir, though of course in a much smaller way for a much smaller reason. Yet Lottegaard was a kind of kingdom to us. And it was a great relief when my son had a little girl." She drew Lotte against her side.

"Of course, after the old man died, Lotte and her lover

were married, and they lived very happily and had eight children altogether. Anders was happy to come back to the land, and he was such a splendid manager that he became known all over Jutland for his fine animals and his good land."

There was a silence. Lotte heard the wind sighing at the window. Now, she thought gladly, Patrick would know how it was with her, and Mor would know why she couldn't leave Lottegaard. Maybe Mor had forgotten lately how it was here.

"And now—" Farmor laid the old paper back gently and the locket with it. "The locket will go on in the family, I hope, no matter what happens to the land and the house." She waved her hand around the room, at the great bed with its lace hangings, at the row of portraits, smiling down. "Perhaps Lotte will want some of these old things. But probably Hr. Axel is right."

"Oh, no, Farmor!" Lotte cried. "Not a *museum*—"

"Hardly. Lottegaard is a *farm*," Farmor said. "But these old things must have better care. You see the silk—it is getting yellow, and now it is beginning to split. It should be in a glass case, as Hr. Axel says, before it falls to pieces." She sighed and laid the dress in the chest once more, in its layers of tissue paper. "People can't go on living on their memories forever, no matter how good they are. Sometime—" She looked at Patrick and Mor. "We must rid ourselves of old things, as the young people say we must. To make place for the new."

Lotte started to say something, but she could not. And Farmor closed the chest gently and turned the key.

CHAPTER THREE

Wedding Festival

Mor and Patrick were married on a blustery March day. Mor did not come to breakfast, and Farmor looked very seriously over her cup at Lotte while Ida fluttered around looking silly and excited. She was making fancy cakes trimmed with silver bells to serve at coffee when people came back from the church. Just breakfast was too dull for Ida today!

Lotte did not feel like breakfast either.

"What's the matter? Stomach-ache?" Farmor asked.

"Ja—"

It was then that Farmor said it. "Lotte, I hope you will be very good to your Mor today. You are the important one to her—you can make it good for her or bad, and I hope—"

Lotte looked down at her egg and swallowed a great dry nothing and said nothing and felt nothing. She had a strange feeling that nothing was true or even there. It was more like reading a fairy story than like waking to an ordinary day.

For a time, Farmor said no more. She ate silently, and Lotte sat and went on eating nothing even when Ida fussed.

"We go to the church at four," Farmor said to Ida, "and will come back, just the four of us and the Gregersens, I

think— Tove will be anxious to get back to the inn—" And
then, at last, to Lotte: "You don't need to eat until you're
hungry. But Lotte, *try*—" And Lotte knew that Farmor
understood. She rushed to her room.

Pastor Gregersen wore his fine collar, and the altar was
beautiful with flowers, even though only two short rows of
friends and relations had been invited to see Patrick and
Mor married. Fru Gregersen and Tove sat beside Farmor
and Lotte in the front row, and behind them were Fru Fugl,
Mor's closest friend, the way Lisa was to Lotte, and then Ida
and Finn and a few others who helped on the farm. The
rest of the neighborhood was coming to the festival. This
was the solemn part. And from the solemn look on Patrick's face, which usually laughed and looked quite different, one would have thought it was a funeral. Maybe from
the look on Lotte's face, too, as Patrick said beforehand with
a chuck under her chin.

It took only a few minutes to be married. Such a big
thing to do in so short a time! Patrick had been working
hard on the Danish of the ceremony, so he could answer
properly, but he forgot once and said in a loud voice that
echoed in the empty church: "Yes! I do!"

Mor smiled, and the next time she said "Yes" too in a firm,
sweet voice.

Then everybody kissed everybody. Ida rushed off to get
the coffee ready, and all the rest of them went back to Lottegaard in the Dollar-Grin.

Somebody had put a huge bow and a pair of cowbells on
the engine. That was Lisa's brothers, Lotte knew; she had
seen them getting it ready.

Farmor squeezed her hand as they drove up to the house. "You were very nice," she said. And then, for the first time, Lotte felt like crying. Did they think she was a *baby?* She rushed upstairs as if she had to go to the bathroom, quick. After a few minutes she felt as if she might be able to swallow one of those nice cakes, so she went down, and when she got her cake, she took the little bell off and put it into her pocket. She would put a ribbon around it and tie it on Lillegris so she could tell which he was, she thought. It was getting so he mixed himself up with his brothers and sisters, and it was hard to tell who he was until he woke up and came to be rubbed.

Nobody seemed to notice her—Patrick was telling the Gregersens about how wonderful Texas was and asking them to come out and visit his ranch—so she decided to go and see Lillegris now. She went out through the kitchen when Ida was busy serving more coffee. But Lillegris was sound asleep, so tucked in and in a heap that he paid no attention to her. Even when she called his name and put her cake, all crumbled, into the trough, he didn't seem to care much. He came with the others, tumbling along, but his mother got the cake. If she could just sit with him, by the fire—if only he would stay little—

Then she had an idea. Her little house—she had never gone there in the wintertime. She rushed through the barn and out the back way, and there was the duckpond, still half frozen, looking ugly and black at the edges. The ducks looked forlorn and raggedy too. How ugly the world was in winter! And there was her tree, her very own tree, with its little house looking plain and perchy with no leaves or blossoms to make it beautiful. She knew it

with leaves and with blossoms around it and with apples
growing gradually sweet. But today ragged vines blew like
a witch's hair in the wind. Old leaves hung on the boughs,
sodden and brown, and the bark was slippery with old
rain and frost. But she climbed up, shivering, and opened
the door and crept inside.

There—she found the lamp she and Lisa had put there,
and the matches too. When she scratched a little light, she
thought of the poor Match Girl because it made a tiny
warmth at once. Everything was rolled up and covered with
canvas, as Farmor had insisted, but she got a cushion out.
The blanket had been taken away, but the doll dishes were
still in the cupboard and an old bear named for *Peter Plyds*.
He was nice, she thought, and held him a little. The pictures she and Lisa had tacked onto the wall were still there,
blown and ragged, and her illustrated poem about this
very apple tree. It still had her teacher's admiring mark on
it and was protected in a small frame. She had printed it
carefully, especially to hang in this place where it had been
written.

THE APPLE TREE

When the world seems dark to me
And I am wondering what to be,
I climb the rugged apple tree.

She had worked for days on the rhymes, and it was nice
when Farmor and Mor bragged to people that she wrote
poetry. But now Patrick said *he* wrote poetry too—even
verses with music to go with them—and everybody sat listening.

Her poem would go to music very well, she thought, be-

cause it was a careful, steady poem with three rhymes in
every stanza.

> Its low branches brown and bare
> Bid me come and nestle there
> And build my castles in the air.

It was a true poem, she thought, and swallowed hard as
she read:

> Many children I could name
> Whose castles are the very same,
> A longing for much wealth and fame.

> But when I think hard, I do guess—

She stopped reading. The "do" wasn't right, but the
rhythm was wrong without it. She could have said, "When I
think hard—well, I guess—" That was better. *Ja,* much
better. She must bring a pencil next time and fix it.

> But when I think hard—well, I guess,
> To have a home for God to bless
> Would bring me wondrous happiness.

Of course she had a home already, but some day she
would have one of her very own. She and Lisa had sat here
many times talking about the houses they would like to
have and what they would be named. They had names for
their children, too—and for their husbands, even if that was
silly. Ole. Maybe, she thought, Ole would go on being the
boy she liked best even after she went to America, and then
she could come back and marry him and live in Denmark
for the rest of her life. Sometimes people married when they

were sixteen. Great-great-great-great-great-great Lotte had—
and that was only five more years. Five years in America and
then she would come back—surely she could manage to
come back if she saved every penny she had. She would
take her pig-bank with her and put every single *øre* into it
and empty it at a bank and fill it again. American money
was big. Farmor said that all the time. She would be almost
old enough, then, to be a university student.

The thought of being a student anywhere but in Denmark
made her feel suddenly sick. Patrick said that in America
students dressed like anybody else. They didn't even get
special caps or go riding around the squares singing and
laughing, with the whole city watching. Imagine—never
to have a student cap of her own!

"Lotte!"

Somebody was calling. Ida. It was time to get ready for the
big *fest* at the *kro*. She shivered but did not move.

"Lotte!"

She sat very still except for her teeth, which chattered
together. But Ida could not hear a small sound like that.
Nobody would dream she would be out here in the little
house on such a cold day.

Silence. Only the wind made a brittle sighing among the
branches. A sparrow landed on the doorsill and did not
even notice her, she sat so still. He hopped in. How pretty
he was!

Come in, little sparrow, come in. You are welcome in my
house, she thought, like a poem. It would be a very pretty
poem, she thought, and leaned to him a little, and he gave
a hop and flew away.

"*Lotte!*" That was Mor herself. She came walking around the house and stood looking. Even though it was only mid-afternoon, dark was settling down. Lotte leaned down and blew out the lamp.

"Lotte!"

Mor walked around calling; it was fun to watch her looking so worried. She went through the brown and ragged garden and disappeared again into the barn, calling. Stillness again. But now Lotte was shivering all over. She moved stiffly out of the door and climbed down slowly and carefully (even to bother Mor, she did not want to fall) and walked clear around the barn and the house and entered by the front door. On the high staff outside, the bright celebration flag was whipping in the wind.

The old *kro* was full of light and laughter and singing. Lotte sat between Farmor and Lisa, right next to the head of the long table. Small Danish and American flags stood at every plate, and in the center of the table was a huge bouquet of blue flowers with red and white candles burning in a circle around it.

"Isn't it *wonderful?*" Lisa kept whispering.

It seemed like hours since food had begun coming. First soup and then roast duck stuffed with prunes and apples and served with red cabbage, as if it were Christmas instead of a wedding. And apple cake with whipped cream on top as thick as the cake, and cheese, any kind you wanted to choose from a huge tray, and then fruit in wonderful designs on huge platters, and at last, with coffee, pieces of the wedding cake, which was full of nuts and fruit. And then candy, mints in red and white and blue, and all the time glasses were being filled with bubbly champagne.

Lisa and Lotte had tall glasses, like everybody else, and theirs were filled all the time with ginger ale that sparkled and sent bubbles up the stem just like the others. With everybody else they lifted their glasses whenever a speech was made or a song sung or a toast proposed. Sometimes the toasts were in English and sometimes in Danish. "A happy journey over the ocean and through all your lives together!" *"God rejse!"* "To happiness and success in America!" *"Til-lykke! Tillykke!"* And of course there was the wish that ends all the best fairy tales: "May you live happily ever after!"

It was exciting to see the glasses lifted all together and to see the guests looking round the table at each other, gazing into each other's eyes. Lisa and Lotte did like the others and now and then touched their glasses together so that they made a ringing like little bells. Their teacher, Fru Fugl, smiled to see them and lifted her glass with them.

With the coffee came small glasses of brandy and great trays of cigars as always at a festival in Denmark. Tove did everything right; she had learned to give a festival dinner when she was a young girl and became the bride of the innkeeper. Now she sat next to Farmor, looking as pleased as anybody and keeping a sharp eye on the waitresses to see that everything was right. Nobody waited for his plate to be brought or filled tonight; nobody must find his glass empty.

Lisa and Lotte had new dresses especially for tonight, and so, Lotte thought as she looked around, did everybody else,

even Lisa's plump Mor, who did not get a new dress every day. She was sitting next to Lisa's fat Far, and they were both laughing and talking and eating huge helpings of everything. They looked happy and settled, as people do who have lived together many years and have had one baby after another. Lisa had five brothers and lived in a comfortable big house called Hyggehuset. Lotte loved to go there where something lively with a big noise was always happening.

Of course, Lisa's mother was not pretty, as Mor was, and she was not young either. Tonight Lotte was not sure whether it was better or not for Mors to be pretty and young. . . . She kept looking at Mor, who had never looked so pretty before. She wore a blue dress that exactly matched her eyes. Her hair had been especially done in Randers, in a beauty shop, and it was golden and high with little pearls laced through. Around her neck she wore Patrick's wedding present. It was a necklace of jewels that sent out colored sparks every time she turned her head. And when she lifted her hand to drink some champagne, her new rings sparkled too.

Yet all of her shining looked rather silly, Lotte thought, when you turned and looked at Farmor. Because Farmor wore the Lotte locket tonight, and it was a firm and steady shining against her dark blue dress. Even though the locket was so old, the jewels were still as bright as new. Everybody looked at it and remarked how beautiful it was. And they knew, because Farmor wore it tonight, that this wedding pleased her and that she meant it to be a great family festival.

Fru Fugl had made a song about "Denmark and Texas,"

and the words were passed around for everybody to sing together. The words were in English on one side and Danish on the other. *Melody: Happy Jim,* it said over the English words. *Melodi: Lykkelige Jim,* it said over the Danish. Outside, on the cover, were the names: GERDA AND PAT, and the date, March 15, 1963.

At last came plates of candy and nuts, and all the grown-ups had coffee in tiny cups. In their cups Lotte and Lisa had chocolate with dobbets of whipped cream on top. Lotte longed to drink it, but she could not. She felt stuffed to the chin. And the candy and nuts—she took some of each and put them into her handkerchief and tied them up to eat later, in bed or maybe the next day on the way to Copenhagen. It was fun to think of going off to Copenhagen—and Lisa was so jealous that was fun, too, if only going did not mean Mor's going. When I come back here with Farmor, she thought, staring at the dobbet of whipped cream and feeling sick at her stomach, Mor will be on the ocean, going farther and farther and farther away. It was still hard for her to believe that Mor was actually going. How easily she had fallen in with the plans Patrick thought were "wise" and that Farmor thought were "right" and that everybody in the whole neighborhood thought were "good." Sometimes Lotte felt that everybody she knew was on one side, and she stood alone on the other. Even Farmor. Even Lisa.

If only Hr. Axel had been able to come to the wedding. *He* would not be on the other side. He had always understood. When she asked Mor whether he could be invited to the festival, Mor had turned a little red. She had answered, "Of course! How nice of you to think of it, Lotte!" And an invitation had gone off. And Lotte had tucked in a secret little note when Mor was not looking. It said, *"Please* come. Did you know that Mor is going to America and I am going to stay in Denmark until school is out? Maybe you can come to see us on the Fifth of May again and help me light the candles in the windows the way you did the last time. Maybe you will have dinner with us in Copenhagen—will you? I asked Mor if I could ask you, and she said we would talk about it when you come to the wedding."

He had answered with a lovely letter on which he had drawn funny little pictures like the cartoons he did for his newspaper. "Dear Lotte! I wish I could come to the wedding, but I am too busy just now. I will be able to see you in Copenhagen, though, two days after. I am writing to arrange it with your mother and Mr. Patrick. Love! Hr. Axel." And he put two silly little hearts around the "love" as if he were in love with *her* instead of Mor. But she knew why he was not coming to Mor's wedding. He was broken-hearted too.

Yet she wished he were here. Somehow, now that Farmor seemed to think it was so wonderful for Mor to go away, he seemed the only friend left. In Copenhagen she would sit by him at dinner, and they could talk, and she knew he would understand how she felt about never leaving Denmark, even though Mor was leaving it. Fru Fugl was saying, in a voice that carried down the table: "Patrick, you are going to sing for us?"

"Ja, ja! A song from Patrick!" Everybody began to chant it, all together.

Every time Patrick went anywhere now, people asked

him to sing and play his big Texas guitar. One of the first things Mor ever said about him, Lotte remembered, was how she had enjoyed hearing him sing here at the inn. "He told us about America and sang old songs," Mor had said that night when she came home. "Odd—I had never thought about America having all those old folksongs. Of course, as he said, a lot of them came from England and Ireland and all sorts of places. He said America is a sort of 'grab-bag'— full of everything and everybody. And the most wonderful songs of all, he said, are the ones the Negroes sing. That's *real American,* he said. They're called 'spirituals,' and he sang them very slowly, making his guitar sound like an organ in a church. 'Spirituals and cowboy songs—that's real American folk.'" Since then, Lotte had heard Patrick sing dozens of times. Fru Fugl had him come to the school one day, and everywhere he went, people insisted they wanted to hear him. Now everybody began to clap. Lisa was clapping her silly hands off again. And he stood up.

"A man shouldn't be asked to sing at his own wedding," he said.

"Why not?" That was Lisa's Far, shouting down the table, laughing until his fat cheeks shook. "If we asked you to *cry* now, Pat, it would be different!"

Patrick looked at Mor, as if he were asking her what to do. She smiled up at him and nodded, looking happy and proud. After all, the people at this festival were her friends; many of them had been Far's friends too, all his life. But they were glad to see her happy again even if it meant she must leave them forever. Lotte felt that she couldn't *stand* to hear Patrick sing. Why must he sing tonight? But there he was, standing with one hand on Mor's shoulder, and everybody was silent to hear what he was going to say. "Some of you made wonderful words to sing to us tonight," Patrick said. "And when I answered, trying a little bit of my bad Danish, you were all kind to me. And I want to say *tak, tak, mange tak, tusind tak* for everything!"

How they clapped! Whenever he opened his mouth to speak Danish, they all acted as if he were a genius or something. He had practiced for days and days with a record player, learning to be married in Danish, and that pleased Mor and Farmor so much that they couldn't even speak of it without getting tears in their eyes.

"It just happens," Patrick was saying, "that I have made up a song too."

Everybody began to clap and laugh. And somebody said, "And it just happens, of course, that you have brought your guitar!"

Patrick had said this before. It was a joke in the neighborhood now. He had been here long enough so people dared to tease him in the Danish way, making fun. And he could tease them back. He had learned that Danes tease only people they really love.

Farmor leaned over to Lotte, as somebody went off to fetch the guitar. "Imagine, Lotte, Patrick has made up a song about the Lotte locket! He showed it to me tonight while you and your mother were getting dressed."

About the Lotte locket!

"It isn't exactly like the real story," Farmor said. "But it's very clever. And I told him I'd be proud to have him sing it."

Lotte felt her back go as stiff as a flagpole along her chair.

Usually Patrick sang American songs, story-songs mostly about big tough men who built railroads and cut down trees as high as the sky. There was one about a cowboy dying down in Texas and another about a poor, lonesome girl whose lover had gone away and was never coming back. He always sang, at the last, a song about how blue the sky was in Texas and how there were never any clouds there, a song that made Danish people shake their heads and sigh for summer.

Now Patrick was looking directly at her and Farmor. "I'm afraid my song touches very lightly on a serious and important family story," he said. "But your songs tonight touched very lightly on serious and important things—marriage and love. This song of mine just happened to come to me when I had seen the Lotte locket for the first time and had heard the story. I began thinking of rhymes to an old tune." Now he had his guitar and stood tuning the strings as he talked. Everybody sat very quiet, listening.

Farmor smiled at him and said, "I think it tells our story very cleverly, Patrick, and I think everybody here will understand."

As always, Patrick began his song by making skippy notes, up and down. He could make his guitar do anything. It could be as deep and sad as an organ at a funeral. Or it could laugh or sing or make you want to dance. Lotte had to confess that Patrick was very clever with his guitar. He said that in Texas he was not considered clever at all, because everybody played guitars and sang down there, most of the people far better than he did—which was hard for Danes to believe. He had learned to play, he said, when he was a boy helping to herd cattle and riding horses and sitting around campfires at night. "That's one of the most American things in the world," he had told them. "It's true, it happens just the way you see it in the movies. Not all you see in those movies is true"—which always made people laugh, for some reason—"but the Western songs are true. We really sing 'em like that when we get together in the mountains or the Texas hills or around fires in our houses after dinner."

He put his head back as he always did when he was ready for the words. His voice was big and fine. This time he went on talking a little, to the music, before he started on the song. "I wish I could have made Danish words to this Danish story," he said. "But that would take years—and my wife"— he looked down at Mor—"she said she was too busy to do it this week. And she said there were too many rhymes, besides—"

How quiet it was, all around the table. Lotte stared down at her cup and stirred at the whipped cream with her spoon. She wished he would stop talking and sing his song and sit down again.

His voice came deep and true, and there had never been a lovelier tune on his guitar.

> "Once there lived a maiden fair
>   Who loved a man as poor as poor,
>   Though handsome, young, and bold.
> 'I've found for you a husband, dear,'
>   Her father said, 'and he is here!'
>   Then came a man in to the door
>   As rich as he was old."

Patrick could make words sound as if they rhymed whether they did or not, and his fingers made trills and runs on the strings between the verses.

> "He loved her and brought finery
> And frills and lace and shinery
> And a satin-lined pocket,
> And hosiery and slippery
> And chests of ruffled frippery
> And a golden jeweled locket!"

Everybody looked at Farmor and at the bright old locket around her neck. After all, not everybody had a ballad written about her locket. Lisa was so excited and thrilled that she reached out and squeezed Lotte's hand on her lap. She looked surprised and whispered, "Lotte, you're cold!" and held tight to the hand, then, to warm it up. Patrick went on singing.

> "She was so lovely when she donned it
> He sat down and wrote a sonnet
> For his wife, his dearest dear:
> 'This locket has your name upon it
> In diamonds, rubies, and a garnet,
> So if you ever have to pawn it,
> It will keep you many a year!' "

Of course, that wasn't the real story, but people laughed and nodded and listened as if they thought it were. But the next part, which was really true, even began to be a little sad:

> "She had everything she wanted,
> For his business was appointed

By King Frederik the Fifth,
And she served him as one sainted
Till he died, though she was haunted
By her love, long disappointed,
And his younger, sweeter gift."

Patrick looked down at Mor when he sang about the "sweeter gift," as if anything he sang about love was for her. She looked up at him, listening, with her eyes very bright and her lips parted.

"They found the good man's will did say:
'I leave my Lotte all, and pray
That she do her woman's duty:
Send for her love without delay
And on their happy wedding day
Put all her widow's black away—
It does nothing for her beauty!' "

Everybody was very quiet now; the song had become serious enough for all its gay tune and its rhymes. Mor had been a widow, too, as everybody was remembering, and then Patrick had come. But her husband had been a young man, not an ugly old one, when he died. He had been a hero, too, who had flown over this very village many times during the war, doing things that had helped to save Denmark.

Yet Patrick had been a flying hero too. Now he sang the last stanza of the song much slower, his fingers making long chords across the strings that gave them an organ sound:

"Thus it was, good times began
For all of Lady Lotte's clan,

> And every first-born daughter
> Wears, according to her plan,
> The locket with her name thereon
> In memory of that goodly man
> Who so adored his Lotte!"

Everybody began to clap. Lotte clapped a little, to be polite, but Lisa and Farmor clapped until their hands stung. And so did everybody else.

Patrick said, *"Tak, tak, tusind tak!"* And his Danish thanks made them clap harder than ever. When the noise died down, he said, "And now, I want to propose a toast. To our two Lottes!"

The clapping had been hard before; now it hurt Lotte's ears as she stood up with Farmor. When the toast had been drunk, and they sat down again, Patrick and some of the others began to chant, "Lotte, Lotte, Lotte!" And everybody knew it meant they wanted Farmor to say something. As she stood up again, everybody became very quiet. Many of the guests had been at the wedding of her only son, here in this very room. If I had to make a speech, Lotte thought, I couldn't make a sound—I would cry—and she reached for Farmor's hand and held it tight.

But Farmor did not cry. Her voice was not strong, like Patrick's, but it was firm and kind and sweet, as always.

"I am like the old man in Patrick's song, in one way," she said. "I believe in the future, not in the past. It is sad, as everybody here knows, for me to think of my daughter-in-law and my only grandchild—my Lotte—going so far away from Denmark." She looked down at Lotte, beside her, and Lotte felt her face go red with every eye upon her. "But I want you to join me in wishing Gerda and Patrick well. I wish them every happiness in the new world they are starting for together. We have decided—" and Lotte knew what was coming and kept her eyes on her lap. "We have decided that Lotte may stay on with me until school is out. She will make a special study of English so that when she starts school in America next September, she will be able to do well and not make us all ashamed. When she goes also, next July, only four months away, I will need all of you to comfort me and come and keep me company sometimes. Since we are thinking so much about the locket tonight, I want to tell you that when Lotte is confirmed, in America, the locket will go across the sea to keep her company. Perhaps it is a new chapter in an old story. Even the Lotte locket is beginning a new life."

Women were putting their handkerchiefs to their eyes, and men were blowing their noses. Lisa reached out and pressed Lotte's other hand.

"And now it is time," Farmor said in her sweet and gentle voice, "for the very old and the very young to say good night. Thank you for coming to wish my family well. And thanks to Tove and her daughters for the splendid dinner and for making everything so beautiful. Even in the old days here, I have never eaten a better dinner. I am glad we could celebrate together tonight where all of us have shared so many sorrows and so many joys."

Mor was wiping her eyes, and Patrick put his arm around her very firmly. People began to clap rather gently as Farmor took Lotte's hand and left the table. And they began to clap harder and harder as Farmor reached the door and turned to smile and wave her hand. She had made the best speech of all.

Patrick came rushing out to say that he would take them home. "Of course not! You mustn't leave your guests," Farmor cried. And he was sent back again, and Lisa's Far came and drove all of them to Lottegaard together. "May Lisa stay?" Lotte cried, and her Mor said it was all right, but she would have to borrow one of Lotte's nightgowns. And so she did. But they were so tired they couldn't even laugh at how long Lotte's nightgown was on little, short Lisa. The next morning, Lotte could not even remember when she got into bed and fell asleep.

She thought she remembered Lisa's saying something about how nice the wedding was. She thought somebody— Farmor?—came in to tuck her in and say good night, but she could not be sure. And there, suddenly, was the sun shining in the window and Ida shaking her and saying, "Lotte! Hr. Patrick says if you don't get up *right now,* the whole lot of you will miss the ferryboat!"

As they dressed and ran downstairs, Lisa kept saying, "Lotte, be *sure* you send me a postcard, even if I don't get it until you're home again. Won't you? Of the Royal Guard. Or the palace. Oh, if only I could go to Copenhagen! Or to America . . ."

"Hurry, hurry!" Patrick was carrying out suitcases. "We've got to be out of here in fifteen minutes, hear?"

Fifteen minutes. In fifteen minutes, Lotte thought, Mor would say good-by to Lottegaard.

"Where on earth is Gerda?" Farmor said. "She's not even come to breakfast."

"She says she doesn't want any." Patrick was looking very serious. "She said she had to go out and say good-by to the barns!"

Of course. Naturally. To the barns, Lotte thought, and the cows and the horses and the pigs and the chickens and the ducks and geese and to all of the pigeons in the cote and the sparrows she fed every day and to the old well in the courtyard and to the house—to her room—to her pretty curtains and to the wheel on the roof where the stork built its nest— And day after tomorrow to Copenhagen. And then, the morning after that, to Denmark. Now she would see maybe—

Lotte ran out the back door to be with Mor when she said her good-bys. Patrick called from the door, "Tell her to hurry! If we miss that boat—"

But Lotte did not tell her. Instead she said, "Mor, you must say good-by to Lillegris. I told him you would." And they went together. He was a lot bigger already, and Ida had said he was too big and dirty to stay in her kitchen.

"There!" Mor said, and her nose was running and as red as it could be.

And out came Patrick and said, "Look, Gerda—" and he picked her up in his arms and carried her through the whole house, from back to front, with her laughing and kicking and losing a shoe. And he put her into the car, with Lisa and Ida and Finn and the boy who milked the cows all standing together, waving, wiping their eyes with their sleeves and handkerchiefs and Ida lifting her apron to wipe her eyes. At the last minute, Lisa gave Mor the shoe she had lost, and then they all laughed and the Dollar-Grin went skidding on the gravel as Patrick turned it around. . . .

Lotte knelt on the back seat beside Farmor and waved from the back window until Lisa was out of sight.

CHAPTER FOUR

❧

Lotte the Guidebook

Lotte kept her nose pressed against the window of the Dollar-Grin. It was steamy inside, but Mor wouldn't have the windows open on account of her bad cold. She had awakened with a cold, she said. But Lotte had an opinion: it seemed odd to her that a woman would cry and cry the day after she was married. Unless she really didn't want to go away on a honeymoon to America.

There was still time to change her mind. The ship wasn't going to sail for two days. When the time comes for Farmor and me to get on the ferry and go home, Lotte thought, looking at the countryside swimming by, she will say, *Pat, bring my suitcases. I am going home. I have decided to stay in Denmark.*

Certainly she wouldn't be able to leave Copenhagen, whether or not she had been able to leave the farm.

"You can always tell Copenhagen when you start seeing the greeny spires," Lotte said, as if none of them knew anything about Copenhagen at all.

Mor looked at her with a smile. "You sound exactly like a guide," she said. "Did you know, Lotte, that Pat lived for almost six months in Copenhagen when he first came to Denmark?"

Lotte felt her face go red. She had mentioned the greeny spires because she knew Mor loved them. They always watched for them on the way to Copenhagen. She had begun to mention all the things Mor loved as soon as they started out that morning because all along the road through the village, people were watching from their windows. Every farm looked beautiful, even though the trees and hedges were still bare. Mor had waved to everybody, and her eyes and her nose ran and ran. And Lotte had started to sing, as she had planned to do, a wonderful old song called "In Denmark Was I Born."

That was when she started being the Guidebook. "That song is by Hans Christian Andersen," she said. "He wrote it, Fru Fugl said, to think about when he traveled in other countries because he always got homesick for Denmark." After that, she hummed the tune every now and then, whenever she noticed especially lovely things along the road that Mor must say good-by to: all the familiar farms and the hills swelling gently against the sky and even the clouds of birds rising as they passed the quickset hedges and the stubby trees waiting for spring. And all the familiar houses, each with its name over the door and the year it was built. They passed Lisa's house, Hyggehuset, 1880, and Mor asked suddenly, "Pat, do people name their houses in America?"

Lotte held her breath because she knew they didn't. But Pat nodded and said, "In Texas we name our ranches the loveliest names. The one where I was born was called Rancho Rio Grande." He put his arm around Mor's shoulders and said, "What shall we name our place? Think of a good Danish name."

The dairy. The mill. Poul's Carpenter Shop. And then, what Lotte had been waiting for especially, the monument at the crossroads.

"I'd like to stop for just a second here," Mor said, and Patrick drew up with a squeal of the brakes.

"It better be a second," he said.

"I meant to bring some flowers," Mor said and rushed to the little gate and stood still, looking up at the tall stone covered with names. Her own brother's name was there and Farfar's name and Tove's husband. So many. They were the heroes who had made this neighborhood famous all over

Denmark. One day the King himself had come here to honor them and had eaten his dinner at Tove's inn.

Patrick glanced at his watch, but he didn't say another word. Farmor sat with her gloved hands folded tight in her lap.

"There—now you can go as fast as you please," Mor said, jumping into the car again.

"And the inn—must you stop to say good-by to Tove again?" Patrick asked, just the least bit cross. "That's *my* favorite landmark, you know—the place I first saw you, and the place I had the greatest *fest* of my life." He actually stopped the car in front of the inn.

"No. No, I said good-by to Tove last night," Mor said. But her eyes were shining now in a different way. "How wonderful it was!" She turned to Farmor as the car went down the road again. "Wasn't it the most wonderful—" But she did not finish. There had been other festivals more wonderful for Farmor, and she seemed suddenly to remember this.

"I've never eaten a better meal," Farmor said in her gracious, quiet way. "And I've never seen a more beautiful table. Or heard better songs." She turned her head and looked back at the inn as it disappeared behind them. It looked quiet and empty in the morning sun, but the flag was out as always when the sun was in the sky. "I do wish Patrick might have known Tove's man. I'm sure he was the best innkeeper in Denmark."

So the inn vanished behind them, and the school. Lotte felt she knew Tove's man well, for pictures of him were in every room at the inn, and he was in all of the pictures of the Danish heroes at school. She knew dozens of stories about him and how he was always laughing and how wonderful he made a festival and how brave he was when the Germans came and how he helped Far and all the others by catching the guns and supplies they dropped down from the sky at night. And how, finally, he and the others whose names were on the monument at the crossroads were kept in jail a long time and then shot, standing against a wall. "He loved to entertain," Farmor had said when she told about him. "The more the merrier. When old friends arrived, he would sometimes forget to put on his wooden shoes, even when there was snow on the ground, rushing out in his socks to welcome them. Every day he put the flag up on its pole, every sunset he took it down."

"One thing he never forgot, Tove told me," Patrick said, "was to present a bill. A practical man. He would say, 'I hate to charge you for your festival, but I must buy for the next one.' Tove said the same when I paid her yesterday."

Patrick was going so fast now that there was Randers already. The tower of St. Peder's and then, whisk! the Square and the House of the Holy Ghost and the Town Hall.

"Did you know," said the Guidebook, leaning her elbows against the front seat, "once they moved the whole Town Hall two whole yards on rollers?"

"They did? Why?" Patrick asked.

Lotte sat back. She didn't know. She looked at Farmor, but Farmor laughed and said nobody knew. As for her, she didn't believe it had happened at all but had been told by somebody like Tove's man, who wanted people to think that neighborhood was the most wonderful in Denmark.

"Patrick, not *quite* so fast through town," Mor said. "You'll be arrested, and then we'll never get to the ferry."

Lotte looked hopefully back for a policeman, but there was none, and they were already out of the town and on the road to the ferry.

"You said I could go as fast as I pleased," he said. "When you get to the States, you'll be used to it. If you went as slow as this on the freeways, you'd get bumped from behind, and a cop would get you for *not* speeding." And then he said one of his awful things, one of the things Lotte had learned to avoid whenever she could by pretending she did not hear. "Lotte, here's another English lesson: we are going 70 kilometers an hour; how many *miles* an hour are we going?" When she was silent, he glanced back and said, "I'll give you a hint—one kilometer is .6214 miles."

That didn't help her one bit. She was not very good in arithmetic, even on paper, and Patrick seemed to expect a person to do problems right in her head.

"There's an awful lot of arithmetic about changing languages," he said, which was not cheerful news or new news, either. It gave her the shivers to think about it. "Kilometers for miles. Centimeters for feet and inches. Hectares for acres, grams for ounces, kilograms for pounds. Can you think of any more?"

"*Kroner* for dollars and *øre* for pennies," she said. And to make him forget about arithmetic she said, "Hans Christian Andersen is on every ten-*kroner* note. My teacher said he was the only poet ever to get put on such an important bill."

"How many dollars in a ten-*kroner* note?" Patrick asked.

Anyway, she knew *that*. One day he had given her a one-dollar bill and a ten-*kroner* bill and said they were almost the same. But every time arithmetic was the subject, she began to feel littler and littler until she was about the size of a *nisse,* a goblin. She was glad when they came to the ferry before he could ask any more questions. They stood in a long line of cars and motorcycles, and a man was coming for their tickets so they had to pay attention. "Just made it," Patrick said. "Well—we breathe again!" And he gave Mor another squeeze and two kisses on her eyebrows and one on her mouth, which made Lotte feel absolutely sick at her stomach, it looked so silly.

Soon they moved forward onto the boat and were tucked in as firmly as a card in a deck. As they climbed out of the Dollar-Grin, Patrick said, "Nothing is more Danish than ferryboats."

"We have Jutland and five hundred islands besides," said Lotte. "We *have* to have lots of ferryboats."

Mor laughed up at Patrick. "Islands are at least *one* thing Denmark has more of than Texas," she said.

"We're thinking of doing something about that," he said, winking an eye at her. "We've got so much land we don't need that we figure we might cut some of it up and put some water between to give us a little variety. Only trouble is we have to haul the water so far . . ."

That was how it was the whole way to Copenhagen. Driving through Zealand, with lovely farms on either side of the road and wonderful old thatched houses everywhere, Patrick taught her to play a game. "This is what my brothers and sisters and I used to play when we had to drive for a thousand miles across Texas," he said. It was fun, especially because everybody who ever played this "car game" had to make up his own rules. One got points for things on one's own side of the road: five points for a thatched house, ten points for a church, one point for a cow. When they passed a man on a horse, Patrick said they should get two points for men on horses. She had to write a list of points to remember all of them. A dog. A cat. "And," Patrick said, "a thousand points for an elephant."

She had to laugh. Who would ever see an elephant in Denmark?

"We thought we'd never see an elephant in Texas," he said, "but one day my brother and I were playing this game and suddenly—on *my* side, wasn't that lucky?—we saw two elephants just walking along. And then two more. And two *more*. It turned out that a whole circus was going into a town, on its way to a parade."

"A hundred points for a windmill!" she said suddenly, after that, for she saw one on her side.

"In summer you could give a thousand points for seeing a stork," Mor said, "they're so scarce now."

"Almost as scarce as elephants lately," Farmor said. "Our wheel has been without a stork family for two solid years, and they always used to come."

"And swans—" Patrick said, passing a lake.

"And ugly ducks," Mor said.

"In Texas, we have rules about Indians and cowboys," Patrick said. "And for buffalo."

"How many for a *castle?*" Lotte asked. That would never be in Texas, only in Denmark. She asked it loud enough for

Mor to hear because some of their happiest times had been
spent visiting castles. There was one not far from the farm
called Clausholm that she and Mor and Farmor had seen
only the summer before. It was hidden in the deep woods
and was so mysterious and shadowy that she liked to think
it was the one where the Sleeping Beauty had lain, long ago.
They had gone inside to look at rooms and rooms, and it
had wonderful pictures all over the ceilings (though goodness knows how artists could paint like that, upside down),
pictures of fantastic animals and countrysides and sphinxes
and cornucopias pouring out fruit and flowers. Even before
the first Lotte had lived, Farmor said, King Frederik IV
came to visit the family that lived at Clausholm and fell in
love with their daughter, Anna Sophie. Soon he came riding
back in the middle of the night and carried her off to Copenhagen to be his queen.

"Five thousand at least for a castle," Patrick said.

"With a moat, ten thousand," Mor suggested.

"And a moat with swans—"

Playing such a game, Lotte didn't even mind arithmetic.
Adding up one's own points was fun, especially because
Patrick said he had a prize for the winner.

"How about a museum?" Farmor asked, because they
were passing one. "And a cathedral?"

"A cathedral is a church," Patrick said.

"Heavens, no!" Farmor said. "A cathedral ought to have
forty times as many points as an ordinary church. I thought
scarce things got the most points, and a cathedral and a
church are as different as a cat and an elephant."

They decided that a museum should get a thousand points

too, being very scarce. The one they passed was a ship museum, like the one in the castle at Elsinore, only of course much smaller. Lotte said, "I wish we had time to go in and see the old ships and the models. Up at Elsinore they have Danish ships that have gone all over the world. To China and to Africa and to Greenland and to the West Indies." Surely it must make Mor very proud to think of how far Danish ships could go.

"The Virgin Islands are still very much Danish, even though they belong to America now," Patrick said. "Did you know that the capital of St. Thomas is named after a Danish queen—Charlotte Amalie?"

When they caught sight of Copenhagen, the game ended, and Lotte had to add up the points. Mor had written them all down on a paper, and in two long columns headed "Patrick" and "Lotte." And Lotte had won!

"Where's the prize?" she asked.

"In my suitcase," Patrick said. "You'll have to wait until I unpack."

Now that they were driving into Copenhagen with a thousand things to see, too many to add up in any game, she did not mind waiting for her prize. There were the greeny-goldy spires she remembered so well. "The tower of Nikolaj Church has golden balls on top," said Lotte Guidebook, "and Our Saviour's has a spiral staircase, and the City Hall is the highest of all and has a clock. And the Exchange has a tower made out of dragons' tails, all twisted together."

"Lotte, Patrick knows—" Mor said, but Patrick interrupted her.

"I want to hear what Lotte knows about her own

capital," he said. "It's amazing what American children
don't know about Washington. Or New York. And I know
people who have lived in New York all their lives who have
never even gone up to the top of the Empire State Building
or on the Staten Island Ferry. *There's* a ferry, now, as good
as any in Denmark." He sent a smile over his shoulder at
Lotte, but it had to be quick because there were lots of cars
to watch out for now and hundreds of bicycles flipping
around like bugs at the corners. "Copenhagen was my first
European city," he said, "and I guess nothing is ever more
wonderful to an American than that. The first one usually
turns out to be the favorite, forever after." Now he risked
their very lives to give Mor a squeeze, just because she looked
so glad that Copenhagen was his favorite city forever after.

"It's good to see your first European city from the—"
Patrick stopped. But all of them knew what he had almost
said. *From the air.* Lotte knew why he stopped. He knew
as well as she did that it was important to keep Mor from
thinking too much about sad things today. It was in the air,
this very air over Copenhagen, that Far's plane had suddenly
gone wrong. Nobody ever figured out exactly what happened. It was just after take-off. Lots of people had died,
but Far had been the pilot. As little as Lotte had been when
it happened, she could remember the man who came to tell
Mor, and she could remember all the people who came, the
whole long day, and how awful it was to see Mor with her
face white and her eyes— Her eyes had been huge, and ever
since, when Lotte read the story about the dogs with eyes
the size of the Round Tower, she had remembered that day.
That was the day Lotte had first met Hr. Axel who had been

sent by his newspaper and who—like Patrick—had been
Far's friend during the war.

Mor's eyes were straight ahead now, and for a minute
nobody spoke. Then she said stiffly, "I think it *will* be good
to live in a new city—to start over where—" And the queer
silence seemed to fill the Dollar-Grin and burst out of the
windows. Mor was so afraid of flying that sometimes, when
an airplane just flew over Lottegaard, she went pale and
covered her ears. "I should get over such a silly thing," she
once said. "But somehow—I don't know—I get weak in
the knees just to think of flying, and my stomach actually
turns."

And Farmor had patted her hand. "We all have such
things, Gerda. It takes time to get over shocks like that.
And you grew up, remember, during the war when planes
meant such terrible things to all of us. My stomach turns
too— I think maybe there are a thousand turning stomachs
under every plane that flies over Jutland."

And now for Mor it was worse than for anybody else, because Far had died in an airplane that had failed.

"I've got rooms in a hotel right on the harbor," Patrick
said, talking extra quick and loud. "How do you like that,
Lotte? I figured you'd like to watch ships under your
window."

She was not sure she did, not now that Mor was going off
on one, but she didn't say so. When they went into the hotel
and were shown to their nice big rooms, she ran to the
window right away to see what was underneath. Sure
enough, there was a freighter, looking as big as ten barns
put together. "Look, Farmor," she said. And then, amazed,

"It's called the *Texas!*" Had Patrick *known?* She stood staring down. Huge cranes were working, picking up automobiles and boxes the size of summerhouses as if they were buttons. The whole harborside was a lively mixup of barrels and sailors and ropes and bicycles and motorbikes and trucks and people and, of all funny things, horses with hats on. It was like an anthill when you stuck a shovel in it. You could watch for hours and see new things all the time. The cranes really did look like huge bugs and reminded Lotte of ants when they carried crumbs and things twenty times their own size. Or when they started to move their eggs down into their holes.

"There's the ferry we'll go on tomorrow night," Farmor said, pointing down the street. "Won't that be fun?"

The office of the ferry company was on the other side of the wharf, and it had huge letters spelling out its name: Det Forenede Dampskib Selskab. Over the ferry there were huge letters saying, DFDS, and then Aarhus, which was where the ferry would take them.

"What long complicated words," Patrick said, "to say something simple like The United Steamship Company!"

He meant it to be funny, like a lot of other things he said about the Danish language, and Lotte was glad he went off to his own room with Mor and left her to watch the harbor by herself. Farmor knew Lotte didn't like what he had said. "Things you learn as a child always seem easy," she remarked, as they began to take her things out of her suitcase. "And you never seem to forget what you learn as a child. Do you know, Lotte, I can recite long poems I learned when I was your age, and for years now I haven't

been able to memorize so much as a new telephone number!"
She came and glanced out of the window over Lotte's shoulder. "I hope you'll learn lots of things, like poetry and quotations from Shakespeare and dates—and languages—" Farmor said. "Now is the time."

Now was the time to learn English better. Lotte knew what she was thinking.

And suddenly there was Patrick again. "Here's your prize," he said.

It was an envelope with four tickets to the ballet for that very night!

It had begun to darken and lights winked in every direction. Ships and ferries with brightly lighted rows of windows went slowly by in the harbor. Lotte leaned on the windowsill and watched and watched. She heard Farmor having a bath and soon she came back, in her robe, and said she had put more water in the tub. "We need a good rest before dinner," she said. "And if we keep up with all the things Patrick has planned for us to do, we'll need a good night's sleep besides."

How different the feel of a city was! After Lotte had her bath and lay in her bed to rest, she couldn't sleep for the wink of the red lights out of the window and all the noises of cars and people. She thought of the nice gentle sounds of Lottegaard when evening fell and wondered if Mor was thinking of them too. Doves would be cooing and cows lowing to be milked, and sparrows would be having a loud singing contest (as Farmor always described them) before settling down for the night. Ida would be making lovely sounds of setting the table and lovely smells of cooking.

There was never any noise on the farm, only *sounds*. She closed her eyes.

But a city has other things, she thought. And Mor loved Copenhagen because she had heard its noises when she was a little girl.

Suddenly she woke and knew she had been sleeping for a long time. Farmor was up and dressed in her nicest dress, and on the foot of the bed was a white box.

"So—you're awake," Farmor said. "Look what Patrick sent us—flowers to wear to the ballet. His 'three generations,' he says on the note, 'are to wear orchids tonight.' "

Orchids! Lotte had never seen an orchid except in shops and the one Mor had worn the night of the festival. And here was one that was her very own. She tore at the string, excited.

"Mine is huge—look at this—" Farmor said. "And yours are small—how lovely they are! I guess your mother will have middle-sized ones—" It was rather like the story of *The Three Bears*. And when Lotte saw Mor in her pretty dress, with middle-sized orchids, sure enough, she had to agree it had been a very clever idea Patrick had. Mor wore long blue and gold earrings that shook with light when she turned her head. At dinner she and Patrick had everyone looking, they were so handsome together, and Patrick made a big thing of getting a bottle of golden wine to match her hair. What a dinner! They had roast duck again, which Patrick said was his absolute favorite of all the food in Denmark, especially for a celebration. Farmor said that she couldn't eat another bite or she would waddle like a duck herself and never be able to get into a taxicab. And then they got their coats and went off to the Royal Theatre, like Cinderella going to a ball, whisk, whisk. And, just as in a fairy story, everything in the Royal Theatre glittered. Lotte thought it must be the most glittery place in the world. In the lobby women were peeling off their warm coats and boots and unwinding their scarves and taking off their hats; underneath they wore beautiful dresses, and they looked exactly like butterflies coming out of cocoons. Everybody seemed to be happy and beautiful. Flowers were everywhere, and when the women moved, they left little breezes of perfume behind them. Huge crystal chandeliers blazed and sparkled, and gilt cupids flew in every direction. There were elegant boxes, one especially fine with a golden crown on top to show it was kept for the King and Queen and their three Princesses and royal guests like the King of Siam.

No wonder H. C. Andersen had loved the Royal Theatre so much that he came there every single night, Lotte thought. Nothing was so exciting as a curtained stage when you didn't know what was behind it, only you did know it would be something beautiful and new. Over the stage was a round, laughing face and a long, weeping one, and the words *EJ BLOT TIL LYST*.

"What does that mean?" Patrick asked.

Mor said, "Not only for pleasure."

But Patrick said, "I know the *words* it means; I meant what does it *mean?*"

Mor looked surprised. "Just what it says, of course. A play —or a ballet or an opera—is for much more than mere pleasure."

Patrick nodded. "That's what I thought, but one of my

friends said it meant different things to different people. So I wondered—"

Lotte hoped to goodness he wasn't going to ask her what it meant, but she felt him looking at her and knew he would. "What do *you* think it means, Lotte? *I* think it means a theatre is meant to teach us good things to learn."

Mor said, "Surely they didn't mean to put a thing as solemn as that over a stage."

Lotte sat staring at the words. For a minute her head seemed to stop working, and she felt all blank as if she were the worst dummy in the world. And then, suddenly, she *knew*. "Maybe it means there's something besides fun in the world," she said. And she was thinking, as she hoped he knew, that there were awful things like his taking Mor off to America—

"Good!" he said.

She was glad the music was starting and the lights were growing dimmer and dimmer, like failing candles. The curtain trembled, and then it rose. And there were the dancers, fairy story people come alive before her eyes. Every single one of them was beautiful; they moved like water flowing or wind blowing, like leaves or petals from a rose bush drifting to the ground. They were not like people at all; they seemed to have no bones, and every minute they made a different picture like colored pieces in her kaleidoscope. The music swayed and swung and beat in time, and the girls in bright skirts moved on the very tips of their toes and whirled, and their legs went up and down, and they leaped into the air, and slim men in brilliant tights caught them as if they were feathers.

It was *The Sleeping Beauty,* one of the most beautiful of all ballets. As she watched she could tell what the story meant—she knew what was going to happen. What a moment, when the Prince danced up to the Princess and leaned down to give her the kiss that would make her alive again!

Maybe, she thought, I could be a ballet dancer instead of a movie star. She would tell Lisa she had changed her mind, after all. Everybody who saw her would say, "That's Lotte of the Royal Ballet!" Mor would say to the people who sat next to her in the audience, "That's my daughter, Lotte. I never dreamed when I left for America, long ago, that she would grow up to be the first dancer in the Royal Ballet!"

Suddenly she thought of Lillegris. Maybe there could be a ballet made up about the swineherd and the naughty princess who kissed him in exchange for a kettle. Lillegris could take the part of the most important pig; how sweet he would look, trotting about the stage with a blue ribbon on his tail. Perhaps he could be taught to stand on his hind legs and walk like the illustrations in *The Three Little Pigs.* Why not?

When the curtain fell, she clapped until her hands ached and stung. They went out with all the other people and had little cups of coffee and chocolate, and then it was all happening again, only it was another ballet, and she fell asleep before it was over. When she woke the lights were bright and everybody was moving out once more. Then they were covering themselves like butterflies crawling back into their cocoons and going off yawning into the cold night. It had begun to rain. Long ribbons of light wound down into the street from every lamp and every sign, and when they got

back to the hotel, the ferry was just moving away from the pier, making a shine on the water all around.

Mor and Patrick were going to a party, as late as it was. "Another supper!" Farmor said she was glad she didn't have to eat it, for she still waddled like a duck from her dinner.

Kissing Lotte good night, Mor said, "Heavens, she's so

tired I doubt whether she'll ever settle down. Such red cheeks, Lotte!" Lotte breathed deep of her perfume and moved close. "Watch out for my flower!" Mor said.

Then they went off, and the elevator carried Farmor and Lotte up and up. Even the elevator boy was yawning.

The strange room felt lonely and cold. The strange bed was turned down very neatly, and the maid had put Lotte's nightgown and slippers on it. She rushed to look out of the window, to see the ferry move away, with the people still waving from the railings to the people on the shore. Longer and longer pathways of light sparkled over the water, and then the ferry disappeared, and all the people went away, and the harbor was deserted and looked sad except for the red letters and the long words that Patrick could not pronounce. The freighter too had sailed off while they were gone.

Farmor came from the bathroom and got into her bed. "Traveling makes me more tired than all the work I could do on the farm in a day," she said. And before Lotte even got her nightgown on, Farmor was making gentle little snores. It felt lonesome when somebody was asleep in a room, Lotte thought. She wished people would stop talking and walking and laughing out in the hall. There were queer noises, the humming that seemed to be in the middle of the hotel, maybe the elevator going up and down, up and down. Water kept running down pipes. Beyond walls and walls, there were voices and sounds she did not know. The wind she knew, though, rattling the windows. Imagine, she thought, and a ripple of dread moved over her at the thought, imagine living in a building in New York City with hundreds and hundreds of people she did not

know. Mor would hate it. Maybe she would hate it so
much that she would turn around and come back after
one day and one night. . . . She got up and crept to the
window. Another ferry, from some other part of the harbor,
went sliding by. Tomorrow night she would be sleeping in
another strange bed, sliding across the water of the Sound
and past Elsinore and Hamlet's castle where ghosts were
said to walk on the battlements. She must be sure to watch
as the ferry went past that castle. She must make a prayer
for old Holger Danske who slept in the dungeon underneath, his arms folded and his beard grown into a table of
stone. He was the most Danish thing in all Denmark, as
H. C. Andersen had known when he wrote a story about
him. There was a belief in Denmark that if the country were
ever in danger, old Holger Danske would rise from his chair
and draw his beard from the table the way King Arthur
drew his sword from the stone. This story was the reason
the heroes during the war, those who fought secretly in
the Underground Army, called themselves Holger Danske.

Once, when they went on an excursion, she had told Patrick about Holger Danske. They had looked at him, sitting
there with his eyes closed and his great beard flowing down,
dressed in a helmet and a coat of mail. The guide said he
had really lived in the eighth century and that he grew to
be seven feet tall and could drink five quarts of mead without stopping to take a breath. He won every battle he ever
fought, even against the giant Burman and Strong Dietrich
from Bern who passed through Jutland with 80,000 horses.
Patrick had listened and laughed and said, "Well, you Danes
have tales as tall as we do down in Texas!"

When they came out of the castle, he had asked her to tell him what the words meant over the crown-work gate. And she had worked hard to figure it out, and finally Mor had helped:

"Step in, if thou be worthy.
I open up my archway
To expose to view the crowned castle. . . .
God grant the King and his descendants eternal rootage
As long as the Sound shall kiss the foot of Kronborg."

"Eternal rootage." That meant, Lotte knew, to stay forever where you belonged, forever and forever. And Mor had explained it, Mor herself, and yet she could go away.

Where, she wondered sadly, had the freighter gone? Perhaps to islands where it was not dark all day in winter, as it was in Denmark, islands where palm trees grew and bananas ripened on trees and oranges and grapefruit and lemons hung like baubles at Christmastime, and one could go out and pick them. Maybe it went to China, where the Emperor lived with his nightingale. Maybe to Greenland, where whales swam and lashed their tails at the ships. Maybe to America, where—

Clocks began to strike in all the towers, bells began to ring. She crept back into bed and lay listening to all the sounds so different from home. She heard Mor and Patrick come home at last. She could hear them talking. They were talking about the ballet. "I'd like to take Lotte to *Coppelia* sometime," Patrick said. "And the first Christmas in New York, we'll take her to the *Nutcracker Suite*. It's always done at Christmas, especially for kids."

So they had ballet in America. And Christmas! Somehow, she had not thought about Christmas in America. It seemed wrong that Christmas was anywhere in the world but Denmark. . . .

Farmor gave a sudden jerk in her sleep as if she were having a dream. Lotte moved close to her, and closer, and closer still.

✻

Lost in Copenhagen

Patrick knew all the old jokes. At breakfast, he said, "Did you hear about the little American girl who had never seen a king or queen except on a pack of cards?"

"*Ja.* I heard it," Lotte said. He had told it to her and Lisa about ten times already. The American girl was disappointed when she saw the real king and queen because she had expected they would have heads on both ends. Silly.

The day was half rain, half sun, and clouds flew like winged white horses among the towers. After breakfast they walked on Langelinie, a path along the harbor, which was the most famous walk in Denmark. By the English Church was the Gefion Fountain, and before Patrick could say a word, Lotte the Guidebook told him all about it. "She was a goddess and her father promised she could have as much land out of Sweden as she could plow around in one day. So she turned her four sons into oxen—see, there they are— and yoked them to that big plow and put them to work." They were pulling so hard their eyes were bulging out of their heads; how their mother was driving them on! "They carved out the whole island of Zealand that one day," she said. "And there's a lake in Sweden exactly the same size and shape, so everybody knows the story is true."

"If we could just get Gefion to come to Texas," Patrick said, "she could carve out those islands for us in no time at all!"

They came to the Little Mermaid, sitting on her stone looking as if her story had just now happened and she was coming up to the land to get her legs. "I've heard sailors say that anybody who climbs down and touches her will be sure to return to Copenhagen," Patrick said.

Lotte looked at Mor, who was staring at the mermaid so quietly, you would have thought she was a statue herself. Suddenly she looked at Lotte and said, "Let's!" And down they went, laughing, and then reached up to touch—

How many times had Mor read about the mermaid in the Reading Chair, Lotte wondered. If only it had turned out differently, she would like it better. For the prince to marry somebody else always seemed too awful when the mermaid had gone through so much for his sake.

They walked out to the Mole, the very tip of the point, and took a boat back again, clear to the square where the Royal Theatre was.

"Who's for one little castle before lunch?" Patrick asked.

They went to Rosenborg, which Patrick said was the prettiest little castle in the world. It stood in a park, but today everything looked cold and sad, even H. C. Andersen who sat alone at the end of a long avenue of trees with a book in his hand. As they stood looking up at him, Lotte felt sorry that pigeons had streaked him with droppings. Such a great man for the pigeons to make fun of! One didn't mind them messing up Queen Caroline Amalie, in front of Rosenborg, who looked very funny anyhow and so fat she must have had on twenty petticoats. And the statue of the fishwife at the market looked natural like that because a real sea gull was always sitting on top of her head.

"The children of New York love Andersen too," Patrick said, looking up solemnly. "Did you know, Lotte, that they saved their pennies and had a statue of him put in Central Park?"

She had not known, and a little thrill went over her to hear it.

"He is nearer the ground there—but he is sitting with a book, and there's a duck beside him. Children climb onto his lap and read the words—"

"Which words?"

"It begins: 'It was summer—' " Patrick said.

"Oh, *The Ugly Duckling!*" She had to admit the children of New York had chosen very well.

Farmor said out of a silence, "My mother saw Andersen several times. He used to take walks around Copenhagen every day, getting ideas for his stories."

Imagine, Lotte thought, Hans Christian Andersen himself just walking around like anybody at all.

"Do you know who he reminds me of?" Patrick asked. "Of Abraham Lincoln!"

Mor burst into surprised laughter, but Farmor looked very serious. "They were both great men and very simple men as well. Maybe all such men look something alike," she said.

Rosenborg may have been a small castle, as castles go, but it was crammed to the towers with the most precious things in Denmark. Patrick bought a guidebook at the door and read, as they climbed the stairs. "There are 9,930 different things to see in this place," he said. "So maybe we won't have time to see *everything* before lunch."

The most interesting things were the jewels. Lotte stood with her nose pressed against a glass case, looking at the King's crown and the Queen's crown and the royal jewels and the sceptre and the sword of state. How would it feel to be a princess like Margrethe, she wondered. Or to be the Queen and think when you were going to a ballet, "I will wear the diamonds tonight," and order some soldiers to take a box and come here and unlock the glass case with golden keys and fetch them back to the palace in an armored car with policemen on motorcycles going before and behind? And to wear a crown? She imagined how the heavy gold would feel on her forehead and the blazing of the jewels, like a thousand stars and a rainbow rolled into one. If she stood a certain way, she saw her reflection in the glass case with the Queen's crown beyond, tangled in her hair. Goodness. To be a princess and think of her own coronation day— But she had heard the Princess was so natural and sweet she might well prefer to wear a little hat.

Mor pointed to a locket covered with jewels. "Lovely. But not one bit lovelier than the Lotte locket, do you think?"

Lotte pushed in close to read the card. Queen Anne of England had given it to her mother-in-law, Queen Sophie Amalie, and it had *two thousand* diamonds in it!

"Our locket has only ten diamonds," Farmor said with a smile. "I suppose it isn't anything to be so concerned about, Lotte, is it?"

It was Patrick who answered. "Value has nothing to do with how many diamonds," he said.

Lotte thought of this as they went from one room to another where the very names on the cards dripped with richness: amethyst, diamond, turquoise, ivory, crystal, tapestry. In one room were two golden cups, one with King Frederik IV's initials all in diamonds. It had been given to the King by Count Holstein, who helped him kidnap Anna Sophie to be his queen. The two lovers had drunk out of these very cups at their wedding.

"This is all too fancy for an American," Patrick said. "The thing *I* like best is Christian V's tin-lined bathroom and water pipes."

Lotte was glad to leave; looking at so many things made her eyes pinch together, and climbing all the winding stairways made her legs ache. Even diamonds could get tiresome. She was glad to get to a pretty restaurant, gay with flags and flowers. A fat waiter came and set an American flag and a Danish flag on their table. He was writing down what they wanted to eat when Lotte heard the band. People at the tables by the windows began to stand up and look.

"It's the King's guard," the waiter said. "They go by at noon on their way to the palace. When the band comes, you know the King is at home."

"Mor, may I go and see?" Lotte hardly waited for an answer. After all, a marching band won't wait. But she couldn't get near the window, so many people were looking, and had to go out onto the steps. Still she couldn't see very well because of the crowd and had to push down through. She knew how to push with her elbows and scrunch down to make herself look littler. There—there they were. Her hat was knocked crooked, but she didn't care. How beautiful

they looked! A soldier in front was carrying a Danish flag, bright red and white and edged with gold. Then the men with their instruments shining in the sun, the horns going and drums beating. They all wore high bearskin helmets and white bandoliers. Then came the guard, marching grandly and briskly, with swords swinging.

A little boy was trotting along with them. He turned and called to another boy, "Come on! They play a lot of tunes at the palace!"

Imagine, Lotte thought, having bands come and play for you while you had your lunch. She wondered whether the King and Queen and Princesses came out to thank them when they finished.

A lady smiled down at her.

"Is it far to the palace?" Lotte asked, gazing after the vanishing flags.

"Not far, only a few squares," the lady said.

Why not, then? She could follow them there and back again. She took one good look at the restaurant with its long windows and elegant front door and began to run. Imagine what Lisa would think—the Royal Guard and the Royal Band at the palace! What if the King himself came out today? It must be an important day or the guard and the band would not be wearing their fanciest uniforms. Maybe the three Princesses would come out on the balcony. She could imagine telling Lisa—first about the band and the palace and then about the ballet.

Somebody shouted at her suddenly: "Watch the light, young lady!"

Oh, dear—she had to wait until the light turned again,

green saying *gå* instead of red saying *vent*. But the second it turned, she ran fast to catch up with the crowd that was surging around a corner. She was panting, and there was a stitch of pain in her side. How far now? It had been a few squares already. But heavens, she couldn't turn back *now*.

There it was. There was the huge square, and the guard and the band marched around and around. They stopped in the middle of the great gray ring of palaces she remembered seeing before. One of the guards marched up smartly to a big door that swung open. He was asking whether the King was at home. She craned her neck, and so did everybody else. The man who opened the door was elegant in a cocked hat and a bright red cape and brown leggings. The band had stopped playing, and there was no sound but the rolling of drums.

But the King did not appear. The music started again, and a standard-bearer brought out a flag. Nobody in the crowd made a sound. It was wonderful. Now the colors were going in. And corner by corner, the guard was changed. The band began marching again, at last, with some more soldiers coming behind, dressed as handsomely as the first ones. At the palace gate was a tiny bright red house, like a telephone booth, but with a pointed roof and a ball on top. Lotte had heard of those and seen them in pictures; they were for guards to stand in when they wanted to keep out of the snow and the rain. Once more she hurried alongside the soldiers, and the band was playing again. The cheeks of the horn players were puffed out, and one wondered how they could find breath enough to march and play at the same time. They were going very fast now. Maybe they were allowed to have their own lunch only when they had finished playing for the King. She could hardly keep up with them. The stitch in her side hurt badly now, even when she kept leaning over. Soon she would see that restaurant. It hadn't seemed as far as this before. How hungry she was! All the good things Patrick had ordered would be waiting on the table.

She was walking on cobblestones and kept stumbling, so she had to watch her step. Once her ankle turned over and she had to limp—how was it she hadn't noticed those cobblestones on the way to the palace? The band turned a corner. There—the restaurant would be just there. She stopped, staring. It wasn't a restaurant at all. It was a bakery. Its windows were handsome with cakes and cookies and buns full of currants and great loaves of bread, white and black. A huge pretzel swung over the door. Odd she hadn't noticed it before. She always noticed bakeries when she was hungry. She could smell it too, as if somebody had just now taken bread from the oven.

Maybe she had passed it without noticing, she had been so busy with the band. She began to run fast again, following the music. But her side still hurt. And now there was another odd street, very narrow, and she stopped, looking up and down. She had never, she knew, seen this street before in her whole life.

Well—she turned and walked back to the last corner. All she had to do was find that square where the restaurant was. It was a big street, not a small one like this. All she had to do was walk and she would come to it. But there was another corner. She turned around and looked up at the towers.

Where was the palace? She could not even remember, now, in which direction the palace was.

Suddenly she felt all alone. Right there on a street that would have been wonderful if it had been the right one, she felt more alone than she had ever felt in her whole life. There were more people than she had ever seen on one street, all walking along happily and busily as if they all knew exactly where they were going. She was the only person in the world who did not know where to go. They went in and out of the shops busily, like ants into their holes, carrying bundles and swinging purses and umbrellas. There were dozens of shops, one tight against another, and they all had different signs and different things in their windows. One had a huge platter; that was a barber shop, of course, like the one in Randers. And one had a big key, and one a bicycle hanging in the air, and there was another pretzel, and there was a huge book, and there was a windowful of flowers and another of silver and another of figurines like those Farmor had on the mantelpiece, all in white and blue. And there—there was a restaurant with long windows. But it was not the right one, she knew that at once.

A scary, empty feeling had started to grow in her stomach.

She stopped walking. Her knees felt weak. She was rattling with cold, and her hat was blowing so she had to hang onto it, and that made her coat hang open. The cold wind made her eyes water, and now her nose began to run as well. If only she had noticed the name of that restaurant, she could stop somebody and say politely, "I am looking for ——————————," and they would tell her where it was. It couldn't be far. Whoever would have thought the guard went home another way?

She tried to make the name of the restaurant come into her head. Patrick and Mor and Farmor had talked about where they would go, and they had mentioned it several times. A queer name, starting with a P. Or was it a B? Somewhere or other it had an L—or did it?

Somebody jostled her, and she began to walk slowly, close to the windows. Maybe she was going in the wrong direction, getting farther and farther away from Mor, Farmor, and Patrick. She stopped once again, and a man, hurrying along, bumped square into her and stopped and said, "Sorry!" and took off his hat. She started to say something, to ask him a question, but he hurried off before she could say a word. If only she had not had to swallow first, but her voice was locked in her throat behind a huge ball of something the size of a walnut. She wanted to cry. But how silly that would be, to stand here on a street in Copenhagen crying like a baby! Noon in Copenhagen seemed very busy, everybody rushing in every direction, hungry and ready for lunch. She slipped into a little alleyway to try to collect her thoughts and get rid of the lump in her throat when suddenly—whoosh!—a bicycle turned in, with a huge basket on it loaded with packages. The boy driving it barely saved himself and his load, turning quickly to avoid hitting her. He shouted at her, shaking his fist and pointing back. "Can't you read?" he cried. *"Adgang forbudt!"* Entrance forbidden. She hadn't noticed the sign at all. But when she went back out, she saw it all right. Then why did that nasty boy come in with his old bicycle? She walked on the street again, and her heart was beginning to beat hard and fast, thinking of how easily she could have been knocked down.

Confused, she stood still against a big window full of flowers and candles. A beautiful window, but she did not care whether it was beautiful or not. Now, even if somebody should be kind and speak to her, she would never be able to answer. Everybody looked as if he knew exactly where he was going and didn't care one single *øre* for anybody else. That's the way Farmor said big cities were, even Copenhagen. New York was worse; Patrick had said so. A man and a woman went by, walking together with their arms linked, like Mor and Patrick. She heard them say a name that sounded like the name of the restaurant she could almost remember. She hurried after them, slipping in and out of the people. But the street bent again, and they disappeared. Maybe they had gone into a shop and she could follow them when they came out again. But she looked in several shops and could not find them.

Suddenly she remembered something that happened once when she was a little tiny child and went with Mor and Farmor to the zoo in Aarhus. She had been standing in front of a monkey that was as funny as he could be. She laughed and laughed and pretty soon took hold of a hand that was next to her. Somebody said, "Well, hello there!" and when she looked up, she found that she had taken the hand of a strange woman, a big, tall, ugly woman with long teeth and a terrible hat. She still remembered how shocked she had been, and how her face had felt queer and wobbling, and how she had begun to cry. The woman had been very nice, after all, and when Mor came, which was very soon, she and the woman had talked together. But the shock of looking up she still remembered. Her face felt exactly the same now, as if it were made out of jelly, and her heart was not down where it ought to be but up in her neck, thumping in her throat. And yet it was thumping in her stomach too. That other time, she remembered, Farmor had been very serious and said, "If ever you get lost, Lotte, you must look right away for a policeman. Or the keeper of the zoo. *Somebody in a uniform.*"

So—that was what she needed right now, of course. A policeman. Or somebody in a uniform.

She looked around, but she really had no idea what a Copenhagen policeman might look like, or where she might look for one. She remembered seeing one in Randers riding on a motorcycle. And once she had seen a picture of a policeman on a horse. But the only horses she could see just now were two pulling a beer-wagon, and they were going past at a brisk trot. How in the world would she ever catch a policeman if she saw one going by on a motorcycle. Wave her handkerchief? Shout *"Stop! Stop!"*? She moved out close to the curb and took hold of a sign that told cars where to turn or something; she needed it to steady her knees. A bicycle came close. *Whish.* And another one, with baskets of packages sticking out on either side. But nobody on those bicycles had uniforms.

Maybe if she really saw a policeman and started to shout "Stop!" her voice wouldn't come out from behind that lump. She tried, just to see, and out came a startled squeak. A woman passing stared at her. Oh, dear. . . . She moved along again, pretending she was not the one who had

squeaked but somebody else entirely. There—this was the
end of the street again, and everybody had slowed down,
for the lights said *vent*. That was it. She could stand here
and wait for a uniform to come along. There—that was one!
A man on a bicycle wore a black and white cap and a bright
red coat. A postman. *He* would know! He stopped for the
light, setting one toe on the ground to hold his bicycle up.
She hurried over to him, but just as she tried to speak, the
light changed to the green *gå,* and off he went. She had
almost gotten hold of his sleeve.

People and bicycles and cars went streaming by like an
endless river. She stood watching for a uniform, ready to
reach out if one came close to the sidewalk, and this seemed
to put her square in the way of all sorts of things—like a
young man with thick spectacles and a briefcase who jostled
her and said, "Sorry!" She saw him turn and look back. And
then he turned completely around. "Is something wrong?"
he asked, and she knew it was because her nose was running
from trying to keep her eyes from running. But she could
not answer at once, and then—instead of saying something—
she started to cry.

"Well," he said, blinking the eyes that seemed twice too
large behind his spectacles, "we seem to have kicked up a
storm."

An old man with a red beard stopped and said, "What's
the matter? Is she hurt?" His face looked all wrinkled up
with being kind.

"Hurt?" another man asked, braking his cycle with a
squeal of tires. "Shall I call an ambulance?"

"No," Lotte cried hurriedly, "it's only that I've lost my
Mor and—"

She heard somebody say to somebody else, "She's lost her Mor!"

A lady with a poodle on a leash stopped and asked angrily, "Who hurt that sweet little girl?" And a man with a girl on a motorbike asked, "Was she hit? Who knocked her down?"

Somebody else said something about her Mor, and somebody else even asked, "Can't she talk?" The man with the spectacles and the briefcase tried to say a word, but a lady in a big fur hat interrupted in a loud voice, "Imagine, all by herself! A *child*—" And the lady with the poodle picked up her dog and hugged him as if to say, "Why, even my little *dog* is never allowed to go out by himself."

It looked like a crowd already, like a fire or an accident. And there, at last, was a policeman. He came right to the center where Lotte stood with her handkerchief in a wet ball in her hand, and Spectacles said, "She says she has lost her Mor."

"Well," said the policeman, leaning down, "maybe we can find her. Where did you see her the last time?"

"At a table—in a restaurant—" and the word went from one to another. "We were just going to have lunch, and the Life Guards and the band—"

"Oh, oh!" They were all nodding and smiling. "The guards! Of course, she had left her lunch to go and see the guards."

"Then it hasn't been very long," said the Poodle Woman. "They went by no more than half an hour ago."

Lotte was surprised. It seemed hours to her.

"A restaurant where the guards pass. Do you remember its name?"

"No. It had long windows—" And then everybody seemed to have an idea what restaurant it might have been. Two women began to argue about what street the guards marched along, and Spectacles interrupted firmly and said, "We don't know whether they were *going* or *coming*—" Then a boy on a bicycle began to laugh, and this was repeated, and everybody laughed together. "Were they going or coming?" Lotte was asked.

"At first going—*then* coming—and they didn't come the way they went—"

How they laughed! Newcomers to the crowd had to be told what the joke was, and a shopkeeper came out to see what was the matter.

A pretty young lady with a basket offered Lotte a cookie. "Chewing always helps me think," she said. "It seems to exercise my brains. Maybe you can remember the name of the restaurant—"

"A Porta?"

"Brønnum's?"

How good the cookie tasted! And sure enough, as soon as Lotte had swallowed twice she had an idea. It was because somebody had asked where she lived, and she answered, "At Lottegaard—in Jutland—"

"She's from Jutland!" The word went around, and everybody in the crowd seemed to have a brother or a sister or a grandfather in Jutland.

"Don't you have any relatives in Copenhagen?" the policeman asked.

She shook her head, and he began to ask, "Do you know anybody—"

And she cried, "Hr. Axel! I know Hr. Axel. He works for *Politiken!*"

It was wonderful to walk along with the policeman, looking so important in his fine uniform with gold buttons and gold braid that everybody let him by. "The *Politiken* building is quite near here," he said. And to the crowd, "Move along—move along—there's nothing wrong here—"

Certainly there was nothing wrong now. Lotte turned to

thank the man with the spectacles, but he had disappeared. And in no time at all she was inside a big building and going on an elevator and there, kindly and concerned, was Hr. Axel himself. "Why, *Lotte!*" he said. "I was just now sitting here worrying about you, and here you are. Your Mor—" He caught sight of the policeman, who seemed to be an old friend. "Her family is at the police station," he said.

Then she got to tell the story for the first time. And Hr. Axel telephoned, and while he was talking another telephone was ringing, and it was the most exciting thing in the world. And in a few minutes there came Mor—and Farmor, looking frowsy with her hat in her hand, like a seeding dandelion—and Patrick. Everybody was hugging and kissing and Hr. Axel said, "I haven't had my lunch either!" And off they went, the policeman too. They went back to the same restaurant, and the fat waiter came rushing over, all upset that everybody had disappeared, leaving the sandwiches—

"We'll have them now," Patrick said.

Lotte had never seen such sandwiches. It was like a party. There were whole platters of *smørrebrød,* every kind you could think of, and the policeman said, "You must have my favorite. It is called a Hans Christian Andersen because it was his favorite too."

He told the waiter, who smiled and nodded and said, *"Ja, ja!"*

Of course a fairy-tale man would like such a sandwich. It was crisp bacon laid like a lattice on thick yellow butter, and on top of this were thin slices of tomato and in the middle a nice big hill of liverpaste with a long tassel of horseradish.

"I heard a little girl was lost," Hr. Axel said. "I always find out what is happening, you know. And I said to myself, 'Lotte is in town today, so, of course, she is the one—' "

"You didn't!"

"Ja, I did. I said to my boss, 'I am the one to write about Lotte getting lost in Copenhagen.' " And sure enough, soon another man came with a camera and another man with a little notebook in which he drew a picture very cleverly. Lotte felt herself swelling out of her chair for more reasons than six sandwiches. In the newspaper!

They all had Hans Christian Andersen's favorite dessert. It was made of buttered crumbs covered with mulberry jam and a big pile of whipped cream. It had a lovely fairy-tale name—Peasant Girl With a Veil.

With all the grownups talking away, still Hr. Axel seemed to like best to talk to Lotte. He asked about everything at Lottegaard, after she had told the story of being lost several times, making it a lot better the second time. "I will be over to see you on the Fifth of May again," he said. "So be sure to save me the date for dinner at the inn."

Then he had to go back to work, and the man with the camera and the man with the notebook and the policeman, too. Mor and Farmor and Patrick kept saying, *"Tak! Tak!"* as if they could not thank everybody enough.

"Now—we all need a good rest," Farmor said.

In the car going to the hotel, Mor began to cry. She held her arm tight around Lotte's shoulders and said, "Pat, if things like this can happen— Really, I don't see—" Her nose was red, and she did not look pretty at all.

Lotte's heart seemed to rise like a balloon on a string.

"How can I go when—" Mor blew her nose into her handkerchief. Her hat was crooked, but she did not seem to care. Patrick looked grim and said nothing at all.

"Nonsense," Farmor said. "Lotte was silly, that's all. This happened with all three of us sitting right there, didn't it? Please remember that this silly girl is not going to be here in Copenhagen while you're gone, but right at home on the farm where she belongs."

Patrick gave her a thanking look. "I'll see that Lotte is never lost in New York," he said. "You won't need to worry about that. Whenever a parade goes marching by, I'll hang onto her—"

And the moment had gone by, and they all laughed, even Mor. As Lotte lay resting, she tried to be sorry she had caused them so much worry and trouble. But she couldn't help being glad instead, since it had all turned out so well. Imagine Lisa's face when she looked at the newspaper . . .

Only very important people, like visiting queens and presidents and prime ministers, got their pictures in the newspaper.

CHAPTER SIX

❊

God Rejse! *Good-by!*

Lying in the harbor, the ship that would take Mor to America looked as high as the Royal Theatre and as long as all of the King's palaces put together. It had long rows of windows and was as white as snow all over except for a flying Norwegian flag and bright colors painted around its smokestack.

"We're expected," Patrick said, as if they were entering a house for tea. "The purser is an old friend of mine, and he said to bring you to see your ship." He was talking to Lotte, and she looked at him in surprise. "You'll sail on this same ship when school is out," he said. And they went up a long gangplank with an awning like a merry-go-round.

So this is how they look, Lotte thought, excited, for she had watched such long white ships hundreds of times from the strand by Farmor's summerhouse. She felt very important when the purser shook hands with them, for he looked like a general or something in his blue and gold uniform. He and Patrick talked about the ship the way men will talk about their machinery, and he showed them fore and aft as proudly as a woman shows her house to a visitor. He showed them the lounges and the decks and a huge swimming pool.

"It is a world of its own," Farmor said. "Think of all this sliding across the sea."

"She is 16,844 gross tons," the purser said, "176 meters long and 22 meters wide."

Lotte pretended to be interested in something else entirely so Patrick wouldn't ask her how many feet, but he figured it out in his own head—"577 feet and 72—" He asked lots of questions and found out that the sea voyage from Copenhagen to New York was 3,372 nautical miles.

"Our last trip took seven days, six hours, twenty-nine minutes," the purser said.

"That's a lot of water away," Mor said.

"Some people prophesied that when there were jets to take them to America in six hours, they would never bother with ships again. But every crossing we are crowded. People will always love the sea."

"Especially Danes," Farmor said.

Mor said quickly, "Lotte must see our cabin." She held Lotte's hand as they went down the stairs. "You will have one like this, Patrick says."

Lotte hoped so. It was a room exactly like those in the hotel, except a little smaller. Mor's trunk sat there, looking at home already, and there were bouquets of flowers with cards swinging from the stems, and two baskets of fruit, and a big box of candy, and some packages with bright ribbons, and a pile of letters and telegrams. "Look at that!" said Mor.

They would be sailing at dawn, the purser said, and must board the ship before midnight. When they walked to the gangplank again, he shook Lotte's hand and said, "I'll be right here watching for you, the sixth of July. I'll take you up on the bridge to see the radar and everything, and we'll go downstairs and see the engines."

Lotte nodded politely, but she was saying to herself that she would never, never, *never,* and slipped her hand into Farmor's when they reached the pier. Patrick and Mor were talking together, smiling, the way people talk when they have a secret. "Lotte," Patrick said, "there's one thing Copenhagen has that is the biggest of its kind in the whole world. Do you know what it is?"

"The Round Tower," she said. Hadn't a czar and his czarina climbed to the top of the Round Tower in a coach and four?

But Patrick shook his head. "I wanted to show it to you. And Mor and Farmor say it's an excursion for you and me."

She was so curious she didn't mind when Mor and Farmor went off in a taxi. "I have one hour before I deliver the car to *her* ship," Patrick said, and she had an odd little feeling about saying good-by to old Dollar-Grin. They rode along Nyhavn, which was a street Patrick said all sailors loved. "It is called Sailor's Paradise," he said. "When I first came to Copenhagen, I went there to dance at that place called The Texas! And I almost decided to get myself tattooed with a mermaid—but I was afraid that someday I would get tired of her, and when something is tattooed onto you, it's terribly hard to get it off." He showed her the little shop where even now sailors were standing in line to get pictures painted on their arms. "A man, people tell me, never feels like a real sailor until he is tattooed," Patrick said. "But do you know who used to live on this street? Hans

Christian Andersen." He showed her the plaques on the walls as they rode slowly by. "If it was as noisy in his time, I don't see how he ever got any stories written." A blare of music came out into the street, and already, so early, sailors and their girls could be seen dancing in The Texas.

Soon they stopped on a street Lotte knew, and she smiled to herself at how hard it was for Patrick to find a space long enough for old Dollar-Grin to be parked in. But he was very clever at parking because, as he said, he had been practicing tucking a big car into a little space since he was sixteen.

"I've seen the City Hall," Lotte said, disappointed, as he led her to the square.

"Just wait. Your mother says you haven't seen *this*," he said.

And it was true. Inside was a sign, pointing to a small room. "Jens Olsen's World Clock!"

"Oh, the teacher told us—"

Patrick was right. The World Clock was said to be the largest and most complicated clock in the whole world. A Danish clockmaker had worked forty years to make it. The teacher had told the story of how he decided when he was a small boy that he would study clockmaking. His sister had read a story to him about an old clock with an eagle on it. When the clock struck the hour, this eagle spread its wings, but one day it was broken and nobody could repair it.

"Why couldn't somebody fix it?" young Jens Olsen had demanded. "If a clock can be built, it can be mended." And from that day on he mended every broken clock and every watch he could find and later on studied all the things a clockmaker must study as well as mathematics and science and astronomy.

The World Clock was set like a jewel in a glass case, and even the Crown Jewels were not more beautiful. It had twelve works, some moving slowly and some briskly, and the man in charge said it told local time and solar time and the time everywhere in the world. It showed where the moon and sun and stars were keeping themselves and what time they would rise and set and when there would be an eclipse.

"One day I stayed here two hours trying to figure it out," Patrick said. "It has 50,000 parts, imagine that."

"Yet it is so simple to care for that it will run for 3,000 years with only a weekly winding of its weights," the guide said, as proudly as if he had made it himself.

An old man stood listening, shaking his head as if he found it hard to believe. "Well, they measure everything now," he said, "even how far to the moon. When I was a boy, I couldn't believe they could figure how far off every one of the stars was from the top of the Round Tower, but now they talk of going up for a visit." He looked at Lotte. "I suppose you'll be going off to the moon one of these days?" he asked.

Everybody laughed, and Patrick said, "No, only to America."

The guide was telling a new crowd of people about the clock. "We are busy on New Year's Eve, I can tell you," he said, patting the glass case as if he and the clock were old friends who worked together. "In six minutes we figure out all the phases of the moon for the new year, and the days of the week for each month. And then we decide when we will have Shrovetide, Maundy Thursday, Good Friday, Easter Sunday, All Saints' Day, and Whit Sunday!"

Lotte walked slowly around, staring at the huge dials and the tiny dials. One showed how the polestar moved around the earth every 25,753 years and one of the hands moved only once around in 7,000 days. There were rings for the planets, showing the different times it took them to travel their circles around the sun. Thinking about all that made you feel as if you were shrinking, like Alice in Wonderland.

The old man smiled at her as if he had read her mind. "I met Jens Olsen once," he said. "He liked children as much as he liked clocks, and he could make any kind of machine you could name. Do you know what he made once on Christmas Eve?"

"No," she said, and thought about how she could tell about Jens Olsen in her next composition at school.

"He always had the neighborhood children in to see his Christmas tree, but he got more and more famous and more and more came. One year it had got so packed in his parlor that the children were like sardines in a can, and when it was time to dance around the tree, there wasn't room. So guess what Jens Olsen did? He said, 'Go out, all of you, and come back again in ten minutes. I have an idea.' And when they came back, he had arranged a clock-work under the tree. So the *tree* danced around and around!"

All the people were listening by the time he finished, and the guide looked rather cross to have his thunder stolen. Patrick made him feel better, though, by buying a copy of a little book he had for sale. "Here," he said to Lotte, "you will be able to read all about it when you are home again. Now we must go.

"One more stop," Patrick said, outside, "before we take the car to its ship. It's just a step around the corner—" He took her hand as they walked, swinging it a little as if he thought he were a boy. And she rather liked the feeling of swinging along with a tall man, even though it was Patrick, and he was soon going to take Mor thousands of miles away. For a minute or two, walking along on Strøget, where cars were not allowed and one could walk right in the middle of the street, she forgot everything but how much fun it was to be in Copenhagen and what fun it would be to tell Lisa about Jens Olsen and the clock and about the Royal Guards and the hotel and the ship and everything. When she and Patrick came to a kiosk selling *pølser,* Patrick said, "Shall we have one? I'm starving." And they stood with the sausage in their hands, catsup and mustard dripping in a lovely mess over the paper and over their fingers. Nothing in the world tasted better than a hot *pølse* on a cold day in Copenhagen.

"And here's my shop," Patrick said. "I want your advice about something I am getting for a present. For a little girl about your age—"

In the shop he said to the clerk, "Will you please show me watches for a girl about twelve years old? Something simple, please, and strong enough to take a few bumps—"

Lotte stood looking at the trays of watches, gold ones and silver ones and big ones and little ones and tiny ones and some for wrists and some in little balls on chains. One could be pinned to a sweater. Some had little jewels all around.

"Do you see one you think will do?" Patrick asked. "She is a very smart little girl—she should have a pretty one—"

She felt a sudden envy for this girl who was so smart. But solemnly she looked at the watches, one by one. "I think she'd rather have one for her wrist," she said. And the clerk took away all but those for wrists. One— She kept looking back at that particular one. It had tiny flecks of gold instead of numbers, very modern and simple, its only decoration a red stone in the winder that looked like a tassel on a hat.

"I think—" She drew a deep breath. "That one," she said.

"All right, that's it," Patrick said. He told the man to

wrap it for a gift so he could take it along with him. While this was done, he looked at watches for boys and bought one of these, also, for his nephew in Texas. "It must be very strong," he said. "I want one of those that can go under-water or be hit with a hammer."

"Nobody would be silly enough to hit a watch with a hammer," Lotte said. "If I had a watch, I'd *never*—" She stopped, blushing.

"Don't you have a watch?" Patrick asked, just as she had expected he would. "Well, maybe somebody will think to give you one on your birthday."

"My birthday is the fourth of June," she said.

He smiled. "I don't think your mother will forget," he said. "And I'll tell her you'd like a watch, shall I?"

She wished she dared to say, "Tell her I like watches like that one with the little red stone on the winder—" but of course she didn't. She pretended to look at other things while Patrick had several other packages wrapped for his Texas relations. "I know," he said, glancing her way as he gathered the small bundles up, "that my nephew is too bright to hit his new watch with a hammer, but sometimes his hammer *slips*." And on the street, as they returned to the Dollar-Grin, he told her about his nephews and nieces and how interesting they were. "When we visit them in Texas next fall," he said, "they will teach you to ride a horse like a cowboy. Maybe they'll try to teach you to ride a steer—"

"What's a steer?"

"The kind of cow cowboys ride sometimes," he said. "And they tie them up with lassos, exactly the way you've seen them do in the movies."

While they waited in a line of people with the ticket that would take Dollar-Grin to America on a boat like the one out of Lotte's window, he said, "I hope you liked the World Clock. Time and clocks always interested me—I used to think of being a clockmaker myself. Do you know where the word 'watch' comes from?"

She did not know.

"It comes from the old time when watchmen used to walk the streets of the towns at night, singing out every hour: 'All's well! Ten o'clock and all's well!'"

She could tell that at school, she thought, when she told about the World Clock.

"I always thought it was wonderful that such a little thing as a watch could tell so much time," Patrick said. "And be right *all the time*. As right as a big clock."

He came to the window and took his turn, and then they walked back to the hotel. They walked along by huge warehouses, and Patrick said, "There are very valuable small things—like watches and lockets. And big things that aren't worth much, but are empty and full of air, like warehouses—"

"And balloons," she said.

"Of course, sometimes the big things are *use*ful," he said. "Like Texas. It's a wonderful place. But I keep thinking about the old Danish saying, 'We are *a very little country, so we must be very good.*'"

It was time for lunch. And then, very soon, it was time for tea and then time for dinner, and it was time for Farmor and Lotte to go down and get on the ferry. All afternoon Mor acted funny, "nervy" as Farmor called it.

"I hate good-bys," Farmor said, "so I hope you and Pat won't stand around and wait until the ferry leaves. I'm tired, and I'm going right down and get into my bed."

They walked down to the ferry, Patrick carrying their suitcases, and Mor held Lotte's hand so tight her fingers began to ache. They went up the gangplank and into a nice little cabin where Lotte and Farmor would sleep. Mor looked pale. And Lotte was glad. She felt sick at her stomach herself and wished, like Farmor, that they would soon go away. But she did not want to go to bed, even though she would sleep in a high bed that she had to climb to on a ladder. Farmor looked up at her when she climbed up to see how it was. "I hope you'll get to bed before I do, or I might get stepped on," she said.

They all laughed, but it wasn't really very funny, Lotte thought. They were all saying funny things, pretending that Patrick and Mor were not really going to get off and go away when the whistle blew. She wanted them to go quickly, and yet she did not want them to go at all. Anyway, not Mor—

Patrick put her suitcase onto her high bed. Then he said, "I have a package for you, Lotte, that you may open at sea. A sort of un-birthday present."

She looked at the huge box; it was about two feet square. It looked like a galoshes box. If only it had been a little tiny one like those Patrick was taking to his nieces and nephews. But there it was. . . . She remembered to say *"Tak,"* though, and made the little bow all Danish children make when they say thanks for a meal or a present.

"I hope you won't be sick, Lotte," Mor said. Then to Patrick, "Sometimes Lotte gets terribly sick at her stomach, all of a sudden—"

"She's a daughter of Vikings, she won't get sick at sea," Farmor said.

"Here's a pill," Patrick said. "Lotte, if you feel sick, swallow one of these, and you'll fall asleep and wake up at Aalborg." He put his arm around Mor and said, "Your Viking-girl will be all right. You know it."

Mor tried to smile. "Speaking of Vikings," she said, "Patrick has to be reminded now and then that America was *really* discovered by Leif Ericson."

"And I read in a Danish history the other day," Farmor said, "that the first known ancestor of George Washington was a Dane named Hvass. He went from Jutland to England about 900 A.D.!"

"Well!" Patrick said. "Then he would approve of me for bringing America a pair of Danes."

"Shall we look around the ship and maybe get a cup of something?" Farmor asked. So they walked around looking at the dining rooms and the shop selling beer and *snaps* and cigarettes and things, and even went down the steep steps to see where the cars and trucks were tucked firmly in. Once Lotte saw Mor crying; she got out her handkerchief and blew her nose.

"I do like the Danish sea names," Patrick said, making talk in front of a map on the wall by the dining room. "Kattegat, Skagerrak, Skagen. They all sound like kicking up a storm."

"Maybe those Vikings named them," Mor said, "before they went up to Valhalla. You know about that great golden hall in Odin's castle, don't you, Patrick? It's the warrior's heaven, and its roof is made of spears and its thatch of shields. And it has five hundred and forty doors, every one of them so big that eight hundred men can come in or go out at the same time, shoulder to shoulder."

Lotte remembered Mor, sitting in the Reading Chair, reading about the Vikings. "When Vikings got killed in the wars," she said, to show how much she remembered too, "they came alive again in time for dinner. And they had a huge pig—they ate pork chops every day, and he came alive again every night—"

Mor put her arm around Lotte, and just then the whistle blew. "Lotte—I—" After all that waiting, it seemed the whistle came too soon now that it had actually come. *"All ashore—"*

Mor kept kissing. "Take good care of everything—of Lillegris—and everybody—"

"All ashore!" Another whistle.

Patrick took Mor's arm. "Come on, darling, or we'll be back in Jutland and have it all to do over again," he said.

"Pat— I can't—"

Farmor said briskly, "For heaven's sakes, go ashore and let us go to bed. And don't expect me to stand by the railing and wave you out of sight—" She took Lotte close against her side. "I'm taking good care of her, and she'll be over there before you know it," she said.

Patrick kissed her, hard on the mouth, and said, "Bless you—" and then they all kissed, Mor a wet brushing and a squeeze that made Lotte think one last time, *Maybe she won't go, after all—*

But now they were gone, Mor calling back, "Come to the railing, Lotte," as if Farmor had not said anything about that at all, and she stumbled on the gangplank, and Patrick held her up with an arm around her waist.

Farmor said, at Lotte's elbow, "I do think I'll go down for a while," and turned away. Lotte almost wished she could go too, for now she was afraid she was going to cry. Or be sick. They were pulling the gangplank away from the ferry now and pulling in the big ropes. She stood by the railing in a long line of people. Everybody seemed jolly and happy, shouting and laughing and even singing with people on the shore. It was very gay and the lights were bright. Beyond Mor and Patrick, standing below in the crowd, Copenhagen was softly lighted, up and down, a fairyland. It was as if she were the one going away and Mor and Patrick were going to stay in Copenhagen forever. But beyond, in another harbor, lay their white ship.

The ferry trembled. It began to move. Lotte saw a line of water begin below where she stood. Wider and wider. Still, there stood Mor and Patrick, waving their handkerchiefs. Patrick kept his arm around Mor's shoulders, and she did not seem to be crying now.

"Bum voyage!" Patrick called. She laughed to show him she had heard. "Bum voyage" was what he called "silly French," which went along with some of the jokes she liked best. He made jokes out of words all the time, especially about how dumb Americans were not to know French or Danish or anything except "Texas-American." Every time there were celery and things at table he would say, "Pass the *horse doors*," just to show he didn't care that French

people called it *hors d'oeuvres.* And when they had thin little pancakes that French people call *crêpes,* he would say, "So—we're having creepies today!"

Now he was making comical signs. Lotte knew what they all meant. He held his nose. That was to tell her that if she fell into the Sound, she must remember to do that and not get a noseful of water the way she had when he took her and Lisa swimming in the sea last autumn. He put a hand on his stomach and one on his back and did a horn-pipe, wobbling his head. That meant he hoped she would be a good sailor. Then he pretended to scribble and nodded toward Mor and put his hand over his heart—she must be sure to write to Mor. And all this time all Mor did was wipe her eyes and blow her nose and wave her handkerchief.

The ferry swung out. The people on shore were getting littler and littler. Patrick and Mor looked like pins. The wind suddenly blew as the ferry turned, and when Lotte brushed her scarf from her face, she could not see them any more.

She turned quickly from the railing. She did not want any of these people to see her crying. And there, like magic, stood Farmor. "I discovered I was hungry," she said. "They're serving tea in the lounge."

From the bright dining room, over tea and milk, they watched Copenhagen harbor slipping by. They saw the bright lights of other ships and masts and huge machines and cranes and beyond these the city towers. Lotte had a huge cup of milk and some cakes and discovered she was hungry too.

"I decided I'd better let you get into bed first, or you'd surely step on my nose," Farmor said.

It was fun to go to the little room with Farmor and look around. A pitcher of ice-cold water was fastened to the wall, and she found a washbasin no bigger than a mushbowl. In a cupboard under it was a funny, old-fashioned pot, in case they needed to go to the toilet in the middle of the night. There were tiny cakes of soap and folded white towels. It was fun to climb the ladder and find herself right against the ceiling.

"Farmor," she called down, "I forgot my present!"

"Imagine *you* forgetting a present," Farmor said.

Nothing is so wonderful as a package, even a very small one. And this one was big enough to hold a dozen things she could think of. It could have held a little drum, even, but Patrick would never give her that. Maybe a little sewing machine—she had mentioned she would like that for Christmas. Surely he wouldn't have given her galoshes. She shook it and held it and measured its weight. It was very light. Something big and light. She couldn't guess, so she started to unwrap it.

Inside, it *was* a galoshes box. Oh, dear . . . but inside of that was another box, all wrapped in pretty paper and ribbon. Well—if anything is nicer than unwrapping one package, it is unwrapping two. This time she untied the ribbon carefully and set it by and took the paper off carefully too, for it was covered with pretty pictures of sailing ships and sea gulls. She could cut them out and pin them on the wall.

"What is it?" Farmor called from her bed.

"I don't know," Lotte answered. "There is *another* box—" This time it was a shoebox. And inside that was another box wrapped in paper covered with Danish flags. And inside *that* was a smaller one still, wrapped in red, white, and blue with a huge bow. So—the present would be very small. She had begun to suspect something, and her heart started to beat harder and harder. . . . The next box was five inches long and very flat and narrow. And a note was wrapped around it, tied with a golden thread.

"There's a letter," she said, peering down at Farmor. "Shall I read it first or open the box first?"

"Open the box, or I shall be asleep and not find out what the present is until morning," Farmor said.

"Don't you know what it is? Honest?" Lotte hated to open it for fear it wouldn't be what she hoped. She wished, *hard*. And then, quickly, she opened the last box. For it was the last, except for a red velvet box that opened with a gold spring. And inside—she sat back on her heels with a cry of delight.

It was the watch. The very, very, very watch.

She scrambled down the ladder to show Farmor. "It's going," she said. "It says five minutes to twelve."

Farmor said, "That's what my watch says too. And my watch is very old, but it is always exactly right."

"Lisa will die, she'll be so jealous," Lotte said. "We've been saving up in our pig-banks for watches."

"Maybe you'll be sorry," Farmor said. "Now you won't have any excuse to be late for anything, ever again."

Lotte climbed back up and looked at the letter. It was written by Patrick and Mor, both, first Patrick's quick big hand: "*Ah Revore,* Lotte. Take care of your Farmor and come to us soon. This watch will tell you the time is passing fast, and then you'll be with your mother again. Love, Patrick."

And Mor: "Darling, I will be thinking of you every time this watch marks an hour. Take care of yourself. Be careful and good and come to us soon."

She lay still.

"How about turning the light out now?" Farmor said

from below. "You can look at that watch all day tomorrow."

There was a switch over her bed, and she flipped it off. Suddenly, in the cool dark she could see the lights along the shore. She should stay awake and see Hamlet's castle, she thought, and wave to old Holger Danske.

"Good night," Farmor said, yawning.

"Good night."

"Have you said your prayers?"

"No. Not yet."

"Shall I listen?"

"No—I'll say them to myself." There were special things to say sometimes, especially tonight. She lay and listened to the water sliding by, and the ferry rocked her bed gently as if she lay in a cradle. But she wasn't at all sleepy. Her legs felt excited, and there were funny bumps in her stomach as if she had swallowed the cakes whole. She *twitched.* "Farmor—"

"Yes?"

"My legs ache."

"All that walking," Farmor said. "Mine ache too."

"It's a funny ache. It's sort of—" She tried to find the word. "It kind of *crawls—*"

"Sounds like growing pains," Farmor said, as she had said many times before.

"I'm not one bit sleepy."

Farmor did not answer. *She* was sleepy. In fact, very soon Lotte knew that she was asleep because she began to make her odd little snort with every breath. Lotte raised herself on her elbow and looked down at the window where lights came and went. The ferry rolled, and behind the fence over the washbasin the toothbrushes and paste slid back and forth as if they were doing a minuet. It would be awful if she flew out of bed, she thought, and frightened poor Farmor. Maybe she would break her arm or her leg, and they would have to send a telegram. "Lotte's leg broken. Come quickly." Now a big light appeared, and she leaned down to see a queenly white ship with wide skirts of light shining around her on the water.

Like the _Oslofjord_. Tomorrow night she would be far out in the sea. A feeling of emptiness came over Lotte when she thought of this, and she thought, Mor is gone. _Mor is gone._ Tears began to run into her pillow. Time had always seemed short before. Now it seemed to stretch ahead forever and beyond that still more forever, like thinking about being dead. She saw time stretching out like a railroad track, and she seemed to be walking along, trying to balance herself, trying to keep straight, but tipping—falling—

Waves slapped the sides of the ferry, and it rolled again. What if there should be a terrible storm on the sea and it should get worse and worse. When they got up past Elsinore and into the Kattegat, they would start rocking harder and harder, and the ferry would lean one way—and the other way—only more and more, and then one huge wave would come, a tidal wave like those she had read about that came sometimes to China and the Philippines. _Tidal Wave Hits Denmark_. That would be the headline in _Politiken_.

She was getting excited, and the funny aching in her legs was worse. Now she imagined the big white ship coming alongside as she was thrown from the ferry on a tower of foaming water. Everybody was being rescued, all around her, but she sank down, and came up, and sank again. Everybody was rescued but her. On the big white ship, Mor and Patrick were standing crying and calling, "Lotte!" over and over into the howling wind. One by one, people were rescued. But not Lotte. Farmor was brought safely to the deck, but not Lotte.

Then another ship was coming, and it was morning again, way up by Skagen, and there Lotte was, floating in the water, hanging onto a beam. Mor and Patrick heard about it on the radio. She was rescued by a lighthouse keeper, and when they arrived, they found her drying herself off by a roaring fire in the lighthouse.

Below, she could hear Farmor breathing steadily. The white ship had disappeared, and she lay once more in the dark. Gently the ferry moved and rocked, and she turned her face into the pillow and slipped her wrist under her ear. What a tiny voice the watch had! And it was saying—she could hardly believe it was true, but sure enough, it was saying, "Lot-te, Lot-te, Lot-te." As plain as plain.

Good-by, Mor, she thought, and a wave of sleep washed over her. And the watch went on whispering gently, "Lot-te, Lot-te, Lot-te."

CHAPTER SEVEN

Of Two Pleasures

A car could get to be like a person, Lotte thought. When she saw Finn waiting in Aalborg with Lillebil, Farmor's old Ford, she wanted to pat it and explain why they had been riding in Dollar-Grin instead, all that time.

Chunkety—chunkety—irk. That was what Lillebil always said.

"Our boat was two and one-half minutes late," she told Finn and held out her wrist. "I could tell *exactly* by my new watch."

"Nobody on that ferry needed a clock today," Farmor said. "Lotte kept everybody up on the time."

Finn said he had never in his life seen such a beautiful watch. "See how long it takes to get to Lottegaard," he said, and laughed and winked. *"Exactly.* My poor old watch has never been sure."

The one thing Lotte could hardly wait for was to see Lisa. And not to see Lisa so much, maybe, as for Lisa to see the watch. "Maybe I could get to school before geography," she said as they came into sight of the village. "It is just ten-thirty-four and geography—"

"Nej, Lotte," Farmor said firmly. "You will wait until

after lunch to go to school, and then you won't be a bother to Fru Fugl. I hoped, Finn"—she pretended it was only to Finn she meant to speak—"that when people got watches, they got some patience too. Because as Patrick said to me the other day, one thing watches have is *plenty—of—*"

"Time." Lotte finished for her. Farmor had said this already about ten times.

The village looked very empty, the way a village always looks, when school is going, to people who are not going to school.

I can't wait until one o'clock, Lotte thought. Geography would be starting in a few minutes. It lasted forty-five minutes. Then everybody would stop for sandwiches and milk, and then they would all be playing games in the schoolyard for a while. If she could ride her bicycle over there about twelve o'clock—

Finn turned to look at her with a secret in his grin. "Lisa said to call her the minute you got home," he said. "She is out of school today. Her mother says she has had a stomachache ever since the wedding, and she can't imagine why."

Lisa home. . . . Before she had time to be pleased, his grin got even bigger and his eyes bluer the way they always did when something pleased him. "It seems that Lisa found something about a friend of hers in *Politiken* last night!"

Politiken. Already! As they passed Lisa's house, she begged to go in. She felt as if she would burst like a rocket if she did not, but Farmor said *"Nej,"* that she would see *Politiken* at home, first, and not disturb poor Lisa until her Mor said it was all right. Finn said, as they turned up the lane to Lottegaard, "The whole neighborhood is excited about your getting lost in Copenhagen. Ida has the paper spread out on the table, decorated with flowers."

She burst from the car, and as she came to the door, Ida opened it. But she did not even stop for a greeting. There—there it was. It was not on page one, but then it was all the bigger for that, since it was not *quite* as important as the story of a woman who had gone around the world eighteen times.

"Look, Farmor—"

Everybody was laughing and nodding and peering at it over her shoulders. There she was, a picture two columns wide, looking quite pretty with a big smile. "But my hat was crooked," she said. It hardly mattered, though, for around the picture the artist had made a tracery of the towers of Copenhagen and of the marching guard and the band. The headline said: LILLE PIGE LØBET VILD I KØBENHAVN, and there was the whole story with Hr. Axel's name on it.

She rushed to the telephone.

"Hello, Lisa!" But it was the operator, of course, asking for the number.

"Welcome home, Lotte," the operator said. "It is a nice story in *Politiken. Ja,* I'll ring Lisa. You must be in a big hurry." She was familiar with the long conversations Lisa and Lotte had over the telephone every day, even when they had just seen each other twenty minutes before. Once she had asked them to hang up while somebody rang for a doctor.

"Lisa?"

But now it was Lisa's Mor. "Lotte, she's just gone off to sleep. She's been waiting and waiting. I'll wake her. Just a minute—"

Lotte tapped a foot while she waited, looking at the paper in her hand. She was more and more pleased with the picture. Whoever dreamed she could look so pretty, even in a crooked hat? She felt as if she were swelling gently inside her clothes, and there was a lovely swimming of pleasure in her head and all over. If only Mor could see!

"Lotte! You're back! Did you see—"

"*Ja,* isn't it wonderful?"

"I got sick right after—"

"I know, but Farmor says I can—"

They both talked so fast they kept interrupting each other. "Mor says it's not anything catching, so you can come—"

"Farmor—" Lotte turned and called loud enough to be heard in the kitchen. "May I go to Lisa's right now?" And into the telephone, "She says '*Nej,*' I have to unpack and get ready for school." Now she did not in the least want to go to school, since Lisa would not be there. It came to her how terrible it would be to go to a school where Lisa did not go. "Well—on my way home, then— *Ja,* I'll hurry—"

"It might be a good thing to hurry and unpack," Farmor said, passing. "And I would like to call Tove if I could find a telephone in this house that wasn't busy."

"Farmor wants the phone—all right— I'll hurry— I've something wonderful to show you— It's a secret. But it's— well, guess then. *Nej! Nej,* it's something we've been saving for, you and I, for *ages. Ja— Ja,* it ticks! I wish you hadn't guessed, but it keeps absolutely perfect time. We tested it by Farmor's watch and the ship's clock, and on the way home I tested it by Finn's big watch. Guess what I saw in Copenhagen? The World Clock! *Ja*—the one we read about —and my watch keeps time as perfectly as all that great, big

clock, imagine that—" And then she said suddenly, "Ouch!"
and laughed and said, "Farmor wants the phone—good-by!
See you right after school. I wish you were going to be
there— Ouch! Good-by!"

While Farmor talked to Tove, Lotte rushed out to show
the newspaper to Lillegris. He did not seem very impressed
when he found the paper was not good to eat, and Lotte
thought, Lisa is better than any pet in the world.

School wasn't so bad, though, after all, even with Lisa
at home. Never in her life had Lotte been so important at
school. Fru Fugl had a copy of *Politiken* posted on the
blackboard, and Lotte had to stand up and tell the story.
"We want to hear it in your words," the teacher said. She
had written the headlines on the board for the English lesson, first in Danish and then in English:

LILLE PIGE LØBET VILD I KØBENHAVN,
DA HUN FULGTE VAGTPARADEN

LITTLE GIRL LOST IN COPENHAGEN
FOLLOWING MARCHING GUARD

After the English lesson, which was the last class that day,
everybody crowded around, and she could hardly get off
down the road on her bicycle.

Lisa was watching from a window. It was so exciting to
tell her everything that Lotte almost forgot, for a while,
that Mor was far at sea. "I'm going to save every single *øre*
of my allowance and get me a watch," Lisa said. "Oh, I
wish *my* Mor—"

"You don't wish your Mor had gone away to America
just so somebody would give you an old watch," Lotte said,

and suddenly the watch seemed small indeed, and she knew she had to go back to Lottegaard and start missing Mor. "I wish I could stay here tonight," she said, "but Farmor said I couldn't. And you can't come over, either—"

But when they telephoned Farmor an hour later to ask whether Lotte could just stay for supper, she said it would be a good thing for them to study together for an hour or so and catch up on their lessons. Lotte might stay until eight-thirty, when Finn would come and bring her home.

Lisa got up and sat in her robe and slippers, and her Mor brought them milk-tea and crackers. It was fun to be at Hyggehuset. When you had five brothers all ages, some-thing was always happening. Palle was seventeen and so clever he was already at the university. Then there was Sven and Knud and Harald and LillePer who was only six, but so bright he could win at a game of Sorte Per every time. Lisa's Mor was almost always in the kitchen cooking some-thing, and while they studied, good smells kept floating up the stairs.

In the middle of the first arithmetic problem, Lotte re-membered something she had thought about on the ferry. "Grownups are *always* asking how old I am," she said. "You know how they do. So I decided I'd figure out a clever an-swer. See—I'm 3,939 days old." That was ten years plus the number of days since her last birthday almost a year before. "And I figured out how many *hours* old I am, too. Look— I'm 94,560 hours old!"

"How many minutes?"

They began to figure all sorts of things, even how many breaths they had breathed since they were born. Or at least up to their tenth birthdays, because you have to date breathing from somewhere. The sum for that one went down a whole page, and Lisa's Mor said, "Well, what hard workers you two are tonight. I thought you'd be too excited to get anything done."

At 20 breaths a minute, they figured each of them would breathe over 96 million times in ten years.

"It's like stars and things," Lisa said.

"My Farmor is eighty—just about. Imagine, she's breathed 762 million times!"

Palle came in and thought he had never heard of anything so silly. But he offered to help them with their English. He had already studied English for eight years in school and had gone with his best friend the summer before on a walking trip through England and Scotland. He told Lotte how to translate Hr. Axel's whole article into English. It was lots of fun to translate a story about yourself.

They had supper in Lisa's room, at a table by themselves, and could hear the shouting and laughing down in the dining room. It was hard to keep LillePer out; he kept coming and clamoring at the door. But finally he came with a message, and they let him in. Farmor had telephoned that Finn was on his way.

"Who needs to be taken home?" Lotte demanded. "I've gone alone lots of times, on my bicycle."

Everybody laughed, and Palle said, *"Lille pige Løbet Vild—"* Now nobody would let her go anywhere alone again for fear she would get lost.

"I could never get lost right here at home," she said. Sometimes the teasing at Lisa's house was more than she wanted to swallow. Those boys were the worst teasers in the whole world, and every time somebody teased somebody else the whole bunch exploded with laughter until Lisa's Mor shouted that the roof would come off. Now, the minute Finn appeared at the door, they all shouted to him that he must keep an eye on her for fear she might disappear behind a fencepost and never be seen again.

"Here is a package Hr. Patrick sent home for Lisa," Finn said, and Lotte looked at it surprised. Of course, she had to stay and see Lisa unwrap it. At what moment she got the sure feeling of what it was, she was not certain, but it was just the size of the last box in her own package. Lisa's hands began to tremble, and she looked up, her eyes wide, when the small velvet box appeared out of the paper and ribbon.

"Maybe it *is*," she said.

It really was. A watch. Exactly the same as Lotte's, only with a blue stone for a winder instead of a red one.

"Now I can tell the time too," Lisa said, enchanted. "Now *both of us*—"

For a swift minute, Lotte had an ugly feeling. It was a feeling of being almost sorry that Lisa had a watch too. She was ashamed when she caught it, there at the bottom of her stomach. Lisa had a Mor; she shouldn't have a watch as well.

"Listen," Lisa said, and read aloud to everybody the note Patrick had put into the box: " 'Lotte chose this for you, so if you don't like it, you know whom to blame. Take good care of her for us, kiss her at least twenty times a day for her Mor, and send her to the boat in plenty of time. Love, Patrick and Gerda.' "

Lisa rushed to Lotte and hugged her hard and said, "Isn't

it wonderful that now we both have watches—*just alike*—"

Lotte was glad to start home behind Finn, the bright light on his bicycle showing the way on the road.

Farmor was waiting. "Up to bed," she said. "I'll fetch up some tea."

So it wasn't nearly so awful as Lotte had expected, not having Mor come in to tuck her up. She and Farmor sat with their cups and some nice cakes Ida had made, and Farmor didn't even scold when crumbs got all over the bed. "You're the one to sleep on them," she said.

She sat in the Reading Chair. "Want a story tonight?" she asked.

Lotte thought at first she didn't, but then she knew she did. After all, since Patrick came, she had got used to going to bed without Mor, hadn't she? "None of the *awful* stories," she said. She didn't want *Little Ida's Flowers* or *The Girl Who Trod on the Loaf* or even *Thumbelina* who had such terrible times before she found her Little Prince. "Maybe *The Emperor and the Nightingale*," she said. That one always made her feel happy at the end, as if death itself had been taken out of the world. Just by one little bird. "Or maybe *The Swineherd*—"

"Make up your mind—" Farmor smiled, riffling the pages. "The only one I *refuse* to read tonight is the one about that boy who killed his grandmother with an axe." Her eyes looked blue and lively in the lamplight, and Lotte knew the stories were only fairy stories, after all. She suddenly thought about how she and Mor had kissed the Mermaid in the harbor. "I think *The Little Mermaid*," she said.

It was an awful story, in a way, though. She lay very

still as Farmor read. She could hear her watch ticking if she put her wrist to her ear, and her thoughts wandered because she knew this story so well she didn't have to follow to know what happened. When Farmor got to the part about the ship sinking, she held her breath. For six days now, Mor would be on the sea. Already, tonight, she was far out on the rocking waves. Farther and farther away every minute. Her heart felt faint to think of it, and as Farmor read about all the terrible things at the bottom of the sea, she felt worse and worse and wished she had decided on a different story. There were polyps down there, stretching out their writhing arms to seize the Little Mermaid. "Every one of them held something that it had caught. The white bones of men who had perished at sea!" She lay curled tight, her watch pressed against her ear, listening to it speaking to her instead of to the words of the story during the bad part. Presently she noticed that Farmor had stopped reading and opened her eyes.

"Not asleep yet? I thought you had dozed off," Farmor said.

"I'm not sleepy at all," Lotte said. She had been counting the ticks of the watch, figuring about the seconds in an hour, the hours in a day, the days in a week, the weeks in a month— And she knew already how much longer some hours seemed than other hours. Sometimes you would think there were six hundred seconds in a minute instead of sixty. Like when you watched Patrick kissing your Mor at the bottom of the stairs—

"Sometimes," she said, "I make up stories while I listen. Did you know that?"

"You do? How wonderful! Did you make one up to-night?"

"*Ja,* I did. It was about a magic watch that belonged to a princess." She had thought of this, all right, and now that she talked about it, it began to grow into a story. "She could stop this magic watch whenever she wanted to. Then everything just stayed the same, exactly the way it was the minute the watch stopped. Nobody got old or sick or anything. Nobody went anywhere else. They all just *stayed.*"

"Where was she?" Farmor asked. "What was she doing?"

"Who?" Lotte looked surprised, for she had been thinking of Mor and not about the princess, after all.

"That princess, of course. What was she doing, and where was she when she stopped her watch?"

Lotte wasn't sure yet. So she said, "The story isn't finished. I'll tell you when I get it done."

"Are you going to write it down? Your mother would like reading a story you made up, I'm sure."

Lotte hadn't thought of doing this before Farmor asked, but now she said positively, "*Ja,* I'm going to write it down tomorrow."

She lay quiet, thinking about the story, and Farmor sat quiet in the Reading Chair, nodding now and then but still not going away, as if she waited for the end of the story to be discovered. "Farmor—"

"*Ja—*" Farmor lifted her head with a jerk.

"Where would you stop a magic watch?"

"If I could stop it anywhere I liked?" Farmor smiled. "Right now, I think. Kissing you good night, right here safe at home."

"With Mor gone?"

"Well—maybe yesterday then." Farmor laughed softly. "You're a wonderful little girl, making up stories. You must tell me how it ends soon, for I think it's going to be very good. It's a regular H. C. Andersen kind of story, I think, don't you?" She turned out the lamp. "Wasn't it lovely, Patrick's sending Lisa that watch?" she asked. "He is a very kind man. It would be a shame, I think, if you decided to stop that watch before he came. Then you wouldn't have a watch, would you? Or Lisa either."

"But I'd have *Mor*."

"Perhaps."

Why perhaps? But Lotte did not ask because she had another question more important just then. "Farmor, did you know about Lisa's watch all the time? Why didn't you let *me* take it to her?"

For a minute Farmor sat quiet in the dark. "Well—I don't quite know. I thought about it once." Then she laughed in her nice, soft way. *"Ja*—maybe I know why, after all. There are Two Pleasures—one is for yourself and the nice things that happen to you. And the other is for other people and the nice things that happen to *them*. I thought you'd like showing your watch to Lisa before she had one. And then you'd have the fun of being happy for her, besides."

For a second Lotte's heart stood still, as it had when Lisa's box was unwrapped. She hadn't been very happy for Lisa for a while. Even now she felt a little sorry that Lisa could brag at school every time she did. Lisa would be asked what time it was as often as she was. And Lisa wouldn't have to ask for the time at all. But then—they could see every little while whether their watches were keeping the same time.

"Good night," Farmor said.

Lotte lay alone once more, in the dark. She thought of the story. Where, she wondered, *would* she stop the magic watch? *Ja*, before Patrick. In spite of the watch and everything, before Patrick certainly. Of course, it was true how lonely Mor had been then; everybody said so. Maybe she could stop it back when Far was alive and all of them lived in Copenhagen. She couldn't remember how that was, really, but it must have been very good; Mor had said so. But

Farmor was here alone, then. Maybe the watch should be stopped still farther back, before the war, when Farfar was alive too, and Tove's husband and all of the heroes. And there wouldn't be any war. Everything would be peaceful—

Then it came to her. *I wasn't here then.* Not here or in Copenhagen or anywhere.

It seemed strange and terrible to think of a time when she had not even been in the world. Where was I? she thought. In heaven, of course, as the pastor said. Then she would have to be born and be little all over again. But if she left the watch stopped, she would have to *stay* in heaven, forever and forever.

It felt very strange, that thought, like a swimming in her head. No matter where the magic watch stopped, somebody would have to be in the world and somebody in heaven. And old. And young. Some would be nothing but skeletons in museums, bones in stone coffins with their clothes falling away like moldy sacks and long hair winding around. She had seen one once, its jointed finger-bones still covered with silver rings. It gave her the shivers to remember, and she reached out and turned on the lamp. She would read for a while and forget that magic watch. She knew she was glad, in spite of everything, that it was now and not some other time. She turned the pages of the book and decided it might be a good idea to read about Ole Lukøje, which was the one Mor read to make her sleepy. He was, after all, the one who put children to sleep and gave them happy dreams under his magic umbrella. . . . I'm glad Lisa has a watch—glad, glad, *glad,* she thought. Farmor was right about Two Pleasures—yourself—the others. . . .

And suddenly Ida was waking her, scolding because she had left the lamp on all night long.

"There's a cable downstairs. Your Farmor copied it out from the telephone," Ida said.

Lotte rushed down to see. HAVING A LOVELY VOYAGE BUT MISSING YOU. CAPTAIN SAYS GIVE YOU HIS LOVE TOO. PATRICK AND MOR.

CHAPTER EIGHT

※

Fru Fugl's Competition

Fru Fugl, Lotte and Lisa agreed, was the best teacher they'd
ever had. When they first said so, Mor had laughed. "Every
year you have the best teacher of all," she said and looked
pleased.

But about Fru Fugl it was really true, even though she
wasn't the prettiest. She noticed everything, and though this
was sometimes bothersome, it made the classroom a good
place to do the right things for a classroom. It was not a
play-place. Fru Fugl would say, when somebody acted silly
or loud, *"Rolig!"* This meant "Quiet!" and you could hear
a pin drop for at least five minutes. Once she said "Fiddle-
sticks!" and explained in English class that this was the same
as "Stuff and nonsense," or as *"Sludder og Vrøvl!"* in Danish. In either language, she could let you know when she
was disgusted.

Or she could say *"Godt!"* so you knew a thing was *good*
in English, or in French class *"Bon!"*

She was one of Mor's closest friends and had been born
right here on the school road. Tove and her husband had
made her marriage *fest,* as they had Farmor's and Mor's
and all of the others in the neighborhood. Her young husband had fought in the war and had died with the other

heroes and lay with them down by the crossroads under the monument. After the war, she had returned to her teaching, needing money and something to do every day, after her two children started to school.

Mor wrote to her, Lotte knew, and Fru Fugl wrote back exactly how Lotte was doing. "I promised your Mor I'd give you special help with your English," Fru Fugl said. "If you would like to stay after school every day—"

But Lotte did not want to stay after school any day. She and Lisa had their best times riding home together.

"Perhaps Lisa could stay with you. There is no harm in improving her English too," Fru Fugl said.

So they stayed. The first day Fru Fugl gave them two books to take home for extra reading, one in Danish and one in English. Nobody would have dreamed, without looking at the pictures, that they were the very same book. In English, *Peter Plyds* was *Winnie the Pooh!*

It was odd—and fun too—to read the same story in two different languages. But Lotte kept postponing reading it in English—too many words to look up, and then quite often they were not in the dictionary at all but only in Peter Plyds's head. Fru Fugl was shocked that she was so slow. "Don't you care whether or not you can read and speak well when you go to America?" she asked, frowning.

Lotte said she did, but sometimes she did not know for sure. English was ugly, she thought. It made her feel tired all over to have to learn a new name for everything—even the flowers that could be expected any day. It was rather nice when the names actually meant the same, like "gold-star" being *guldstjerne* and coltsfoot being *følfod,* and cornflowers being *kornblomst*. And iris was just iris in both languages! And so was a stork. But a lilac was *syren*. And a duckling was an *aelling* and an owl an *ugle* and a *spurv* a sparrow and a *drossel* a thrush!

"Anyway, they behave the same, no matter what they're called," Lotte said one day, as she and Lisa walked by the pond behind Farmor's barns. The ducks waddled and swam with their tails waggling, and suddenly they were upside down.

One morning the first *løvetand* bloomed in the lawn, and Fru Fugl said it was dandelion in English. A lion's tooth. She could see how nearly alike the names really were.

"Why should a pansy be *stedmoderblomst,* though? And in England *heartsease?*" Lotte did not know about stepmothers, but step*fathers*— Nothing in the world was as strange as language from one country to another. Some days she felt lightheaded and dizzy with the thousands of words in the two dictionaries as they lay side by side on her desk.

She was glad one day when Fru Fugl seemed to forget about languages and think about something very Danish indeed.

"Sometimes," she said, looking very serious and gazing up at the Danish flag on the schoolroom wall, "we tend to forget the meaning of things. Even our flag gets to be a kind of habit—up it goes and down again every day, and we don't give a thought to *why*. Even at Christmas, we decorate our trees and make presents and wrap them and cook roast duck and pudding and dance around the tree singing songs—and even light Christmas candles without a thought for the real meaning of Living Light."

She had said this before last Christmas too, and all of them had felt a bit scolded and so had taken care to think very seriously about it until they got too excited to remember.

"Why do we put candles in our windows the night of the fourth of May?" she asked, leaning forward in her chair. She had a way of pointing a finger straight at somebody to get an answer, and this made Lotte and Lisa laugh. Her finger could look exactly like a pecking beak, and her eyes were sharp and quick, just like a *fugl* in a bush, darting from row to row.

Almost everybody raised a hand. Lotte snapped a finger (which she knew Fru Fugl didn't like) to show she knew the answer for sure. But Fru Fugl nodded to Ole, Tove's grandson, who sat in the back row because he was taller than anybody else in the room. All the other hands went down, as he stood up. He would be sure to get it right.

"When the war ended—" he began.

"What war?" Fru Fugl's voice was sharp. *"When* did it end?"

"Well—" Ole's face went red. "The last war. In 1945." Everybody breathed easier when he said the words in a strong, sure voice. Fru Fugl was too sharp sometimes. Maybe, Lotte thought, she was thinking about her poor husband who had died because of that terrible war.

"Ja," Fru Fugl said, nodding. "Go on, Ole."

"When the Second World War ended in 1945—on the fifth of May"— Ole paused to get everything exactly right in his mind—"some people in Copenhagen were so glad to hear the good news that they put candles in their windows, just as they did at Christmas. Other people noticed and thought it was a good idea. The word spread and soon every window had a candle. By night the word had spread around Denmark, and everybody in every town began lighting windows. It was so beautiful that people have done this ever since on the eve of the Fifth of May."

"Godt!" said Fru Fugl. "Good! *Bon!"* She looked at the flag once more. "I want every single one of you to think about the meaning of the Fifth of May when you light candles this year, just as you did on Christmas Eve. And I have decided that to make all this very clear to you"—her eyes looked more like a sparrow's than ever—*"I am going to give a prize."* She paused to let them buzz a little. "I will give a prize to the student who writes the best composition about the meaning of the Liberation. You may tell the story any way you like." She looked at Ole and then all around the room. "Perhaps Ole will want to tell what his grandfather did. Or perhaps you would rather write about the parade we have each year, to put flowers on the monument. Or about the Liberation Museum in Copenhagen. Or—" Now she looked very serious, even sorrowful. "Or about the terrible price the world has paid for peace."

The room was still, as if they might all be reading, in their minds, the familiar names on the monument. Fru Fugl did not have to say *"Rolig"* the rest of the day. When all the children had marched out, she came to Lotte's desk, where she sat with *Pooh* and *Plyds* side by side. "Do you think you could write your composition in English?" she asked.

"Oh, no!" Lotte had never felt more shocked. It was hard

enough to read English without writing it. And it was hard
enough to write a composition in Danish, let alone in a new
language entirely.

"Anyhow, you could write in Danish and then try to
translate it for your Mor and Patrick," Fru Fugl said, and
Lotte glanced at Lisa, knowing how awed she would be at
the very idea.

"I can *try*," Lotte said, but doubtfully. You had to try for
Fru Fugl, no matter how hard it might be, and her heart
felt like a bagful of stone at the thought of what lay ahead.

"I wanted to tell you something secret," said Fru Fugl.
"I have asked an old friend of yours to be the judge of the
contest and come to give the prizes!"

Hr. Axel. Lotte's heart rose again. So he would come for sure. He had come to speak at the school the year before on Liberation Day and the year before that. Everybody loved him, not only for himself and his gay ways and his teasing tongue, but for the kindly things he wrote about the neighborhood and the strong, admiring things about the heroes.

As she repeated the Danish and English words of the lesson, Lotte kept remembering Hr. Axel's visit the year before. She had been so certain that he and Mor were in love. After dinner at the inn he had come out to help them light the candles. They had laughed and talked and, when the candles were all burning, had walked out to see how beautiful the bright house looked from the road.

Farmor had said, "When our son was flying out of England, dropping guns and supplies—and even a man once or twice—how we wished we could put candles in our windows to guide him! Sometimes he flew very low—"

"It was very dangerous, those days," Hr. Axel had said.

And Mor had shuddered at the thought of her husband (not her husband then, of course) when he was a very young man flying low over the swamps and houses, looking for signals on the ground. It was an exciting story, as Fru Fugl had cause to know. Dozens of men risked their lives to go out and get the things that were dropped, and the men in the planes risked their lives too. And in the end, many died, as the monument proved.

"I'm going to write about the fliers dropping guns and things," she said to Lisa, as they came to the monument. She dragged her toe on the road and stopped her bicycle near the little fence that stood around the graves.

"Everybody will write that," Lisa said.

"Maybe. But Ole will write about his grandfather, and I'll write about mine. And about my Far."

"I'm going to write about Patrick," Lisa said. "He flew over here, too. He told us, remember—"

"He's not Danish. You shouldn't write about *him,*" Lotte said.

"But he didn't have to fight for Denmark, did he?" Lisa asked. "He was in the R.A.F. long before America came into the war, just because he *wanted* to. And I think—"

"We ought to write about Danish heroes." Lotte flung the words back, pedaling off so fast that Lisa had a hard time catching up. They didn't mention the contest again that day. But Lotte told Farmor about it at supper. Lotte was just telling about Hr. Axel being the judge and how nice it would be if he came to dinner when the telephone rang. Ida called Farmor, and she talked for a long time. Her soup was cold when she came back, and Ida had to heat it again.

"That was Tove," Farmor said. "Ole has just been over to tell her about that contest."

"Ole was the one to tell what the candles meant," Lotte said. "He'll write about his grandfather—"

"Not if Tove has her way, he won't," Farmor said.

Lotte blinked in surprise.

"Tove has called Fru Fugl and asked her not to have that contest," Farmor said, looking very serious. "She says we ought to let children forget all that and not remind them. And I must say she has a point."

Before Farmor finished her soup, the telephone rang again. Tove again. Lotte could hear Farmor's part of it. "Maybe you're right—*ja,* of course, I see—" When she hung up finally, she said she was going over to the inn. Tove was having some of the women over to see what they felt about the contest. "She says she has tried very hard not to teach her grandchildren to hate the Germans, and if they start reading and writing about all that, they can't help but learn it. So—"

Farmor put on her coat and hat and stood waiting for Finn to bring the car around to the door.

"Sometimes, Lotte, it seems to me that children learn hate no matter what we say or do, as I told Tove," she said. "Do you remember when you were a little girl and all those crows were in the garden? You came running in and said to me, 'Farmor, there are *German birds stealing everything in the garden!'* "

Lotte did not remember it, but she thought it had been a clever thing for a very little girl to say.

Finn honked, and Farmor was gone, calling back, "Get your homework done and into bed by *nine*—hear me?"

In her room, Lotte looked at the windows. On the eve of the Fifth of May she would have candles burning in each one. Hr. Axel would be there, if— She wanted the competition to go on, she thought. Very much. Tove was right about many things, but Fru Fugl was right this time, she was sure. I wouldn't write about hate at all, but about the heroes, she thought. About how brave they were, and about how cleverly they hid the guns, and the men who were sent down from planes in the dark of night. She knew about the man who had been kept hidden at Lottegaard for weeks and weeks until he finally escaped to Sweden under the coal in a barge. She had heard lots of stories, and when she thought about it, she could see that if Tove did not want the children to feel any hatred, these stories should never have been told.

Here in the neighborhood, everybody knew who the heroes had been. Every year the stories had been told, so why should they not be written? Maybe Tove was sorry for some of the things she herself had repeated—about how the tall strangers had come tramping into the inn demanding service and how her daughters served them without a word or a sign and would then brush off their clothes as if the Germans had infected them.

Everybody knew who had helped the Germans, and their children were still ashamed. But the children of the heroes— like little Niels whose grandfather had been a carpenter and was known to have refused to fix anything or to make anything for any man or woman who collaborated with the enemy. Hr. Axel had written such stories in his paper when he came before. Surely Tove remembered that. Downstairs in Farmor's scrapbook, right now, were the stories Hr. Axel had printed in his paper. She went down to find it among the books on the shelves in the study.

"I talked with the women who lost their men," Hr. Axel had written. "There was Thoger's Ane who lived at the mill, which her son managed now. 'My Thoger always had a quick answer,' she said to me, looking very proud. 'Always yes for his friends, but always no for those who gave to the enemy. They used to come in their hob-nailed boots and tramp through the mill and take every grain they could find, leaving nothing for us. So we hid all we could under our beds and once even inside our pillows.'

"And Johan's wife, Maria, told me how her good man had played the violin. 'He used to play at the inn, very loud, when the Holger Danske had things to say to each other out in the kitchen,' she said. She sang for me a song composed by an American, Richard Dyer-Bennet, who wrote it about the resistance in Norway. But it got to Denmark very soon, though nobody knows just how. 'We would sing it at the festivals, as loud as we could,' she said, 'and the Germans did not seem to understand why we laughed. They hadn't enough Danish to follow the songs. Sometimes our loud singing hid the sounds of the planes over the swamp.'"

Hr. Axel had printed the words of the song, and Lotte remembered hearing it sung at Fifth of May celebrations. It was full of interesting rhymes that went to a gay tune. She read it, thinking the music with the words:

"This is a story of passive resistance,
  Of a man who refused to give Nazis assistance.
  A farmer there was, in occupied Norway,
  Who found a grim warning tacked onto his doorway.
  It read: 'You have failed to come up to your quota.
  Next week, if you fail by a single iota,
  Your farm will be taken and you will be killed!
  This is the law and must be fulfilled!'"

It was as rhymey as Patrick's Lotte song but, of course, much more clever.

"The farmer replied: 'Sirs, the undersigned begs
  To inform you concerning my quota of eggs.
  I posted your notice right where the hens live,
  But the stubborn old bipeds still failed to give,

So I wrung all their necks, the foul saboteurs,
Delighted to serve you, sincerely yours!' "

That was one of the wonderful jokes about the war, Lotte knew. Whenever that song was sung, people sat smiling, and then somebody would tell another story of when Nazi soldiers asked their way and people would shake their heads and pretend to be stupid. Nobody would give a direction to any German soldier in the whole of Denmark, so they went on the wrong roads and had all sorts of trouble. Boys hung the wrong signs on the wrong roads, so that soldiers wishing to go to Aalborg arrived in Aarhus or perhaps in a tiny village by the sea.

A favorite story was about the King himself, old King Christian, who rode his white horse on the streets, quite freely, unguarded, every single day. On the morning of the Occupation, April 9, 1940, the Danish flag was down on his palace, and a German flag was up. He called the chief German officer and said, "The flag flying out there must come down, and my flag must go up at once!" And the officer said, "I have orders." And the King said, "Then a Danish soldier will climb up and pull that Nazi flag down and put mine up!" And the officer said, "Then we will have to shoot your soldier." The King stood very straight, for all his years, and said firmly, "The Danish soldier will be myself!" So out he went. But, of course, they did not dare to shoot the King— and after that the Danish flag flew over the palace every day.

Did Tove, she wondered, think they should not tell those old stories or sing those old songs any more? Tove herself had told many times, in Lotte's hearing, how they would listen to the radio in secret, sometimes hearing The Voice of America, and when they heard trucks on the roads, how quickly they would hide the radios, even under the mattresses of their beds.

"The wife of the greatest hero of this neighborhood, the innkeeper, summed up the feelings of all the wives when she said, 'Everybody helped in his own way. Fiddlers fiddled, carpenters built boxes to hide contraband, farmers hid food for the secret prisoners who waited to go to Sweden and for their neighbors as well, though they could charge their friends little and could sell for high prices to the officers." A bricklayer (whose grandsons were in Lotte's class at school) used to carry guns under his loads of bricks and trowels and sometimes hid them in walls he was building. A veterinarian (whose son still came to see Farmor's animals when they were ailing) was very active at night because he was always being called out to visit sick animals, and the Germans did not suspect him. He carried guns and boxes here and there under his supplies. Once an escaped prisoner lay hidden a half-day under a calfskin, after the veterinarian had been stopped and searched—

What exciting stories! Lotte's skin prickled to remember them, especially the story of Ole Geisler, who had been the one to come to the neighborhood and organize in secret. He had been far away (some said in China!) when he had the first news of the occupation of Denmark and was wild with worry about his parents on their farm at home. So he went to England in order to help with liberation. Later he was set down by parachute to organize the Underground, and his name, now, belonged with the heroic name Holger Danske.

Lotte's own Far had known Ole Geisler, but Mor never wanted to speak of it. If Far had not learned to fly, perhaps he would still be alive, working here on the farm where he belonged.

But no, Lotte thought, he would have worked with the heroes here instead, and so he would likely have been dead anyway, lying down by the crossroads, dead of a bullet instead of a crash.

Lotte had heard Tove tell how her husband met Ole Geisler one night at the inn, not dreaming who he was. He was anxious in those days to discover something he could do to help his country, something besides "sitting about hating myself and those soldiers on every road." One night he had come into his bedroom with a strange look on his face. Tove told it wonderfully, her face red with pride: "He said, 'Tove, there are some things coming down by parachute a few miles from here; they need somebody to receive them. But it is very dangerous, I am told, to get those things.' And I answered, 'I cannot see any way for a Danish man but to harness his little dabbled one to the wagon and go out and fetch those things.' "

Hr. Axel had written that for the paper. He wrote wonderfully, every word exactly right. One could tell he knew about words in every line, and Lotte knew that he wrote poetry as well as the things for the newspaper. He had written a poem for Mor one time, and that was the day she had known he was in love. Many men had written poems for Mor, and no wonder.

In this very article about the Liberation, Hr. Axel had mentioned poetry. "Poetry and music are great weapons

when times are difficult. It is sad they cannot take the place
of guns and bombs so that good fiddlers and good poets
might go on living instead of lying dead by the roadsides."

He had been thinking, then, of the great writer Kaj Munk,
she knew. Munk had been killed, too, in another neighborhood that helped the Holger Danske to save Denmark. Now
everybody in the world honored his name and read his
books and went to see his plays performed. "In this neighborhood," Hr. Axel's story went on, "lived one of Denmark's
greatest poets, Steen Steensen Blicher. He lived long before
the Second World War, of course, and walked in peace on
the heath by night instead of having to watch for enemies
there or for contraband from the sky. Known as the Heath
Lark, he wrote a great poem about the bravery of Jutlanders,
a poem so popular with the Underground that it may be
said this poet did more than his share long after his death.

> " 'The Jute does not come out of his door
> Until real trouble strikes,
> Then he does not go in again
> Until he has chased it away!' "

Reading this, Lotte trembled with pride. Many times she
had visited the grave of the Heath Lark, for he had been a
pastor in a church not far from the farm. One could easily
walk there on a sunny day. It was a happy thing that her
Far lay in the same churchyard—though she wished, sometimes, he had been put by the heroes where he belonged. He
had died later, of course, but he had been a hero, neverthe-
less. He, too, had been a Jute and a Holger Danske.

And I am a Jute girl, she thought. All of the Lottes,

every single one, were Jutes. Perhaps one should say a Jutess.
She must ask Fru Fugl. And suddenly she had an idea. It
was such a wonderful idea that she felt her heart start up,
like a bird's. *I will write a poem for the contest.*

A poem. A beautiful, beautiful poem. Everybody would
think a poem should have the prize—if there was to be a
prize. Especially Hr. Axel, who thought poetry was so important. Oh, if only Tove did not put a stop to the contest. . . . I will tell her about the stories and the pride, she
thought, and rushed to get a notebook and a sharp pencil.
Then she sat against the pillows in her bed and thought of
what her poem must say.

First of all, beautiful words, of course. *Love,* she thought.
Poem. Land. Lovely land. But, of course, "There Is a Lovely
Land" had been written already. Everybody knew it, and
everybody sang it for every celebration. . . . She remembered the words over the gate of Kronborg: *"Eternal rootage*
as long as the Sound shall kiss the foot of Kronborg."

Suppose, she thought, I should write such a beautiful poem
that everybody in Denmark would learn it and a great com-
poser would set it to music! It would be translated into every
language in the world, like the stories and poems of H. C.
Andersen and Mor would see it in the *New York Times.*
"Patrick!" she would call, leaping up from the breakfast
table in surprise. "Here is a poem by Lotte! A beautiful
poem about Denmark!"

The next day she would hear it on the radio, all day long,
and when she turned on her TV, she would see a picture of
Lotte and the farm, and the music behind the picture would
be "Lotte's Own Song," the words appearing under the pic-

ture, with a little bouncing ball to show when each word should be sung. "Why, my own little girl . . . think of it . . ." Mor would say. And then, "Patrick, she loves Denmark so much that we cannot ask her to come here. We will go over there and live on the farm. Why not?"

Lotte heard the front door open. Farmor came slowly up the stairs and paused at Lotte's door. "Not asleep yet?"

"Farmor, I had to know about the competition! What did—"

"It's all right," Farmor said and came in. "Tove told me after the meeting that she was glad the whole thing happened—it made us think a little for a change."

Relieved, Lotte looked at the list of words she had written.

"I see you have Axel's stories out," Farmor said. "We were talking about him—Fru Fugl had a letter from him and read it to us. He wondered about the contest, too, at first and felt the way Tove did—the world must forget war now and think of peaceful things. But all the same—" She turned the pages of the scrapbook and paused at the picture of the parade reaching the monument, of the King putting a wreath on the stone. "It's true that to teach children pride in their country, we must teach them about her heroes. And how shall we teach them about the heroes unless we teach them about the wars? Fru Fugl made some very good points, I think—Denmark is so little that we can afford to glory in our heroes and fly our flag and nobody will worry, she said."

"She said that to us, too." Lotte did not particularly like that point about Denmark being so little. "And she said the children in Germany should learn all about what happened, too, so it wouldn't happen again when they grow up—"

"People need pride for the good and shame for the bad, or how will they know which is which? She made a point of that," Farmor said. "She made a very good speech. I was proud of her." Noticing Lotte's notebook, she smiled. "Are you writing something already?"

"Just some words. Today at school Fru Fugl told us something else I liked—not about the contest. It was in science, but it was almost like the idea in the poem—'In Denmark Was I Born'—" She tried to remember exactly how Fru Fugl had said it. *"We're actually made out of the soil and the water of the country where we live.* When we eat the fruit and the vegetables and the wheat in our bread—and the animals—"

Farmor laughed. "That's one kind of patriotism," she said. "No harm in teaching that."

"Ole made a clever remark about it," Lotte said. "We're stamped like a piece of silver or a piece of porcelain—*Made in Denmark!"*

Farmor sat in the Reading Chair. "Maybe we should read a while and put you to sleep," she said. "You're too excited tonight."

"Ja, ja, let's. About Holger Danske, maybe—that's the first story in the book—" But before Farmor could find the place, she was off on another idea. "Ole said he was going to write about the lion General Eisenhower brought to Copenhagen. And about how angry the Germans were when the American and Danish flags were flying at Rebild Park every Fourth of July. He said Patrick was proud about that —he went straight up to the park to see where it happened. The Germans couldn't see how the flags got put up—they

guarded the place and everything. But somehow every single Fourth of July, there they were!"

Farmor nodded. "It's a good story, and after the war, ten thousand Americans came to celebrate the first Fourth of July—imagine, clear from America. Did you know that?"

Lotte lay listening to the old familiar story.

It was nice for a grandmother to be reading about a grandfather telling the old story. "An old grandfather was telling his little grandson all this about Holger Danske," the story said, ". . . and while the old man told his tale he sat carving a large wooden figure, intended to represent Holger Danske and to be used as the figurehead of a ship. For the old grandfather was a wood carver. . . . He carved the Danish coat of arms on Holger's shield—three lions and nine hearts. And he said proudly, 'It is the most beautiful coat of arms in the world. The lions mean strength, and the hearts mean gentleness and love.'"

Farmor paused, smiling. "You're right, it's the story for tonight," she said and read how the grandfather explained "there is another strength beside the strength of the sword." There were books and statues, and there were great astronomers like Tycho Brahe, who peered at the sky from the Round Tower. "He could use the sword, not to cut at men's flesh and bones, but to carve a plainer path among the stars of heaven . . ."

Lotte lay with her eyes closed as Farmor read the ending: "The ships sailed past Kronborg . . . but Holger Danske did not awake however loudly the cannons roared, for they were only saying 'Good day' and 'Many thanks.' There must be a very different kind of shooting to awaken him."

Farmor turned off the lamp and stood up. Lotte's eyes flew open. "Hr. Axel *is* going to be the judge, isn't he?"

"*Ja*—and there will be three prizes. I'll tell you about it in the morning."

"Tell me now—"

"In the morning. Because if you get the proper amount of sleep, I don't see why you shouldn't write as well as anybody in that school. But if you don't—"

"Was Lisa's Mor at the meeting?"

"*Ja*—and her Far too. And do you know what Tove said tonight when I left? She said you and Lisa remind her every day of how it was with her and me when we were girls together, right here. She says she watches you go by almost every day."

"Sometimes she asks us in for cookies and milk."

"*Ja,* so she said." Farmor stood in the warm darkness. "She said tonight—friends weather many a storm together in this life. But they dance many a dance together too."

Lotte lay awake a long time. Now and then she turned on the lamp, for beautiful new words would come to her, and she had to write them down on the list. Her poem would be made of the most wonderful words she could think of; she would string them together like pearls on a golden chain. Like amber—

Pearls. Golden. Chain. Amber.

Once she turned on the lamp to write "Earth" and "Heaven." I'll go to look at the monument after school tomorrow, she thought. She wanted to read all of the names again and feel the special feelings she always had there. The same strange and wonderful feeling she had whenever she

visited Far's grave and helped Mor make it look pretty—
and put on flowers—

When she dreamed at last, it was of her class singing and
singing and waving hundreds of flags that blew in yellow
candlelight. "There is a lovely land . . ."

Eternal rootage. Strength. Gentleness.

Lovely land.

Lovely—

CHAPTER NINE

Lotte the Poet

"I want to stop at the monument today," Lotte said, after school, putting her books into her bicycle basket.

"Me too," Lisa said, knowing why.

They often stopped by the little iron fence that surrounded the monument, but they didn't often go inside along the graveled path and read the words and the names of the heroes. Today Lisa said, looking up gravely, "I'm glad I'm writing about the heroes."

Lotte was silent. Even if Lisa told her every single word she was writing, she herself was not going to mention the poem. She would show it to Farmor, when it was finished, because nothing ever seemed *really* finished until Farmor had read it. She fastened her eyes onto Farfar's name on the stone. Only a poem could make words wonderful enough for heroes, and if she were the only one in the class to write a poem, surely she could win.

"Palle says nobody could possibly have an idea as *different* as writing about the Americans who helped," Lisa said. "And Fru Fugl said one thing Hr. Axel wanted was 'originality'—that means to be different—"

"I know what originality means," Lotte said. Sometimes Lisa gave her a pain, acting smart like that.

"Of course you do—I didn't mean—" Lisa knew why Lotte got suddenly cross. She always did when the Americans were mentioned. But as Palle also had said, who could blame her for being angry at somebody who took her own Mor thousands of miles away?

"I'm going to end my essay with a quotation from General Eisenhower," Lisa said. "First I'm going to tell about the fliers who helped, and then about Rebild Park and the flags, and then end about peace and friendship in the world, see— and put in what Eisenhower said in *The Reader's Digest*. Palle found the article. It's called 'An Epidemic of Friendship.' "

"That sounds good." For a minute Lotte felt a stab of envy for Lisa's idea. But even the story of Rebild would be better if Lisa could write poetry.

Another bicycle was set against the fence just then, and they turned. Ole. He came through the gate and stood with them, and without a word got out a notebook and pencil. "I tried to remember *exactly* what it said. But I couldn't. And I've read it millions of times."

"Not *millions*," Lotte said and wished at once she hadn't said such a thing. Just because she was cross at Lisa didn't need to make her cross at Ole, too. She liked him better than any other boy at school.

"I decided to try a *poem*," he said, glancing at her in a questioning way. He knew she was the only one in class who wrote poetry. "Are you doing a poem?" His question was direct and nice, not smarty or anything, yet she felt her face getting hot, even before Lisa excitedly asked, *"Are* you, Lotte?"

"I don't know. I haven't decided." Why did she lie?
"Come on, Lisa," she cried and rushed out of the gate and
jumped onto her bicycle and pedaled so hard her feet were
going around like the blades of a fan. She didn't even bother
to say good-by to Ole. Until she got to Lisa's gate, she didn't
even turn around to see whether Lisa was following her.
She was, but far down the road. When she came up, panting,
Lotte said, "Let's ride on to the churchyard, shall we? It's
a nice day to ride."

"All right—if you won't go so fast—" It was odd to Lisa,
who was always nice and easygoing, how Lotte could go
suddenly wild the way she did. But she was getting used
to it lately. Now it seemed perfectly natural that Lotte
should want to go on to see her own Far's grave by the
church; after all, he had been a hero too, even though he
was not shot like the others. Lisa had gone with Lotte before, many times, and with her Mor too, to put flowers on
the grave and to clip the grass with shears and to pull the
weeds. The churchyard was a pleasant place on a sunny day,
a good place for a picnic in the sun or in the shade of the
tower. Every grave was kept neat and pretty, winter and
summer; even the very oldest ones were never neglected.
There were stones that had been there for hundreds of years,
and it was interesting to go around reading the names and
what the people had done in the world. There were farmers
and sailors and carpenters and thatchers and doctors and
pastors, every kind of person who had ever lived in the
village. Most of the women had been *Husfru,* housewives,
but there was one that said *Amme.* A nurse. And *Laerer.*
A teacher. On H. C. Andersen's grave in Copenhagen, Lotte

knew, it said *Digter*. Maybe, she thought, that is what
it might say on my grave— A poet. The stone over her
father's grave was a simple boulder and had only his name,
the dates of his birth and death, and the word, *Flyver*. A
flier. A small flag always stood in a small metal stand, but
the one there now was tattered with wind and faded with
sun and rain. She took it out and said, "Tomorrow I'll bring
a new one."

"All the soldiers will get new ones on Liberation Day,"
Lisa said.

"I want to bring this one myself." Lotte stood with her
head bowed and her eyes closed for a minute, as she had
seen Mor do many times. She used to feel very strange and
strong, watching Mor at this place; it was as if Mor were
willing Far out of the ground as she thought of him, how
he looked, how his voice sounded. Right here, Mor had told
many stories about him, about how she had first met him
and how she knew at once that she would never love anybody else, all her life.

Lisa said, breaking the silence which made her uncom-
fortable, "Let's ride by the swamp, shall we?"

Lotte agreed at once. Certainly today was the right time
to visit the historic place. The heath in that spot was surrounded by a beechwood, and square in the middle was a
bog known only to the men who had hunted in that neighborhood all their lives. There they received and sent signals,
and there, until it was safe to move them along the roads,
they could sink the boxes that were dropped from the sky.
Lotte knew the story very well, and she could not count
how many times they had played Holger Danske, she and

Lisa and some of the others. Hr. Axel had printed it in his newspaper, too, when he told the heroic story of Liberation Day.

"They would lie flat with their small radios and listen to the words from the circling planes. *Pay attention—listen again—pay attention—listen again—* That meant *tonight at moonlight . . .*"

Almost every man in the neighborhood became a member of the secret Holger Danske, with the central place the old inn, Hvidsten Kro. Those who did not, those who were against active resistance for fear of what the Germans would do, were never again really respected in that place. "After dark," Hr. Axel had written, "they would come secretly out of their farmhouses and walk over fields and meadows to the secret swamp. They knew every foot of the land; they had lived here all their lives. Sometimes, when the night was empty and the coast seemed clear, they might joke softly and laugh together. But when the moon rose, there was a dead silence. On a solid place out on the heath, they would light three red lanterns and a stronger white one, throwing light in the direction of the wind.

"They thought they heard a whir from the clouds—a faint buzzing. The plane came down, gliding. They saw the hatches open, and small parachutes with containers and one large one with a man came down in the white light. It was fantastically beautiful and strange!"

How exciting it was to think about, especially when one's own Farfar had been one of the heroes and one's own Far had flown in the plane overhead! Next to the inn was a red house that Ole's Farfar had built for his daughter and her family. It was there the parachute jumpers were usually taken, to be hidden and fed and cared for in secret until they could be spirited away to deliver their messages and work with the Holger Danske in other places. Sometimes, soon after they were taken to Copenhagen or to Aalborg in secret, a factory or a railroad or a shipping yard would be suddenly blown up, and the Holger Danske would smile at each other and know they were doing good work.

Once a German plane had seen the signals on the heath. It circled down and around for a long time. As soon as they could, the men put out the lanterns and lay low, but the plane circled the whole neighborhood for a long time, buzzing the houses like an angry bee. To hear Tove tell it! "It went away at last, but then came the German cars and jeeps, filling the road, going here and there. Our men buried everything they had in the gardens, under the bushes. How they did dig! And not a moment too soon, for German soldiers came to search every house and every barn.

"Later they heard the English plane come, but nobody dared to give it a signal that night, and it circled for a time in vain. And then, suddenly, the German plane was back again and chased it away, far over the North Sea."

Again and again, such dangerous things happened. And at last they were caught. Somebody betrayed them one dark night, and they were surrounded. Then they were taken away to jail, and one terrible day, they were stood together against a wall and shot as a warning to the rest of the country. And after the war, they were brought home in their coffins and buried at the crossroads, and the monument was raised up one Fifth of May.

Sometimes Lotte wished that her Far might have been

buried with the others at the monument. But if he had died with the others, so soon, she herself would never have been born. A strange thought, never to have been born.

Lisa shivered as if she had the same thought or another as worrisome. "Let's go. I'm cold," she said.

At school the next day, Fru Fugl said she would give them special time to work on their essays. "Of course, you don't have to enter the contest if you don't wish to," she said. "That is understood. But those who do not write an essay on the Liberation must write one on another subject for composition class."

Lotte took out her notebook and began to write down her list of beautiful words, thinking hard about her idea. When Fru Fugl came slowly along the aisle, watching the students at work, she was trying to decide the things that had to be decided about writing a poem. How many lines in a stanza? How long should the verses be; what plan would she have for the rhymes? A sonnet was too hard, she had tried writing some of those. Four-line stanzas were the easiest.

It was good to have the idea. She began to think about how it could be said. "They say that I am Motherland," she thought, "and Motherland is me—"

Before she could begin to write it down, Fru Fugl stood by her desk, looking at the list of words. "Are you studying your English?" she asked. "Or your spelling?"

"English," Lotte said, and suddenly she had an idea that would make it true. And besides, it would throw Fru Fugl off the scent entirely so that when a poem came in she would be surprised. "I thought it would be nice to translate a poem for practice," she said.

She couldn't have pleased Fru Fugl more if she had tried for a month. "That's wonderful," she said. "The best practice in the world. But you'll find it hard when you come to rhymes. Do you have any poem in mind yet?"

"*Ja*—" Lotte thought of one very quickly, one of the old hymns they sang often at church. She wrote the first line:

"Tusind Aar stod Kristi Kirke . . ."

It was easy to put that into English: "A thousand years stood Christ Church . . ." And the next line,

"Tusind Aar vort Dannevirke . . ."

Ja, it was the rhyme that would be the trouble. She chewed at her pencil. It was fun, trying to make the same words and ideas into two different languages . . . but hard. Imagine how smart those people at the United Nations must be; they translated speeches into every different language you could think of, just like falling off a log. While the speaker was going on with his speech, they told what he had said. Would she ever know English as well as that, she wondered? *Nej,* it was too hard, too many words entirely.

Fru Fugl came around once more and smiled at her work. She sat down and helped for a while. The idea had to be changed just a little, sometimes, for the sake of a rhyme, she said. And later, in English class, she showed what Lotte had done and said, "You see why it is good to learn another language, for then you can read poems in the language the poet used to write it. A poem is never the same when it is put into a language alien to the poet—"

Poet. Poet. Poet. The most beautiful word of all! That, Lotte thought, as she sat writing in bed that night, is what

I want on my tombstone. There was a wonderful story about
H. C. Andersen and how important he thought the word
poet was. He was visiting a great lady, an actress, and she
asked him to go on an errand, to bring her some flowers.
"I will be so happy to have a bouquet from the hands of a
poet!" she said. That was the first time he had ever been
called a poet, and afterward he said, "From that moment I
knew to be a poet was my destiny . . ."

The pencil moved firmly into the first stanza, as she wrote
in Danish this time.

> "They say that I am Motherland
> And Motherland is me.
> When I was young I wondered
> However that could be,
> But now I understand quite well
> This wondrous chemistry."

There. What a wonderful rhyme. Maybe it was a mistake
to start with three rhymes, but if she worked hard she knew
she could do it. She had done it in that old poem about the
apple tree. The last rhyme—"chemistry"—that was especially
good, because it wasn't just common like "love" and "above"
and such words. It sounded rather like a poem by a sad
woman-poet named Dickinson, who had lived in America.
How beautifully she had written of things she had never
even seen—

> "I never saw a moor
> I never saw the sea:
> Yet know I how the heather looks,
> And what a wave must be.

"I never spoke with God,
    Nor visited in heaven
    Yet certain am I of the spot
    As if a chart were given."

Lotte could not imagine never having seen a moor or
never having seen the sea. But she might write, if she chose,
about a building a hundred stories high and how awful to
look down on the birds! Thinking of the American poet, she
thought how much the idea meant to a poem so that, if it
were wonderful, even little words like "sea" and "be"—such
easy rhymes!—could seem marvelous and fresh and new.
As good as the half-rhymes that followed, almost. It would
be quite impossible, she knew now, to make Emily Dickinson into proper Danish, for her language was as important
as her ideas.

She looked once more at her own idea. She must get it
into the poem—or written beautifully in prose at first, perhaps—and then she would make the rhymes. But right away
it began to fall into the rhythm:

"Rainstorms crumble Danish stones
    Into farming land—"

That was almost the way Fru Fugl had said it.

"And into miles and miles of heath
    And dunes along the strand . . ."

She did not quite like "miles and miles." It sounded as if she
repeated one word to make the rhythm come right. Maybe
it would be better to say, "Into miles of empty heath." There.
That was right. It read just like talk, and that was what

made poetry right. She knew from reading it aloud ever since she could remember. You could always tell when a poet put something in just to make the rhythm or the rhyme come right. And now what else in that part? She went slowly through the alphabet to find a rhyme that might fit the idea. *A*nd, *b*and, *c*and, *d*and, *f*and, *g*and, *h*and—*hand*. She wished that she had not started with three rhymes. Could a poem be written with three rhymes in one stanza and only two in another? Maybe—she could ask Fru Fugl. But if she asked a question like that, Fru Fugl would know she was writing a poem. Ole didn't care who knew he was writing a poem; he told everybody and asked questions before the whole class. But if a person told she was writing a poem and then it shouldn't be good—

Hand. Maybe. But the idea. "On every hand . . ." Maybe. *Ja, ja!* Suddenly she had it and wrote so fast that she could hardly read her scribbling:

> "Into rolling hills and woods
> of beech on every hand."

The rain did not exactly make woods of beech. But then— *ja, ja,* it did. Beeches were made of Danish soil and water just as vegetables were, and fruit. And people.

She read the whole stanza aloud to herself. And then the first one and then both together. Maybe this poem was going to be very short, she thought, and it did not matter, really, for sometimes a very short poem was better than a very long one. Emily Dickinson made poems with only one stanza quite often. And so did Robert Frost. And so had H. C. Andersen. . . . Sometimes four lines could have such a big idea that it was a bigger poem than a sonnet or even a saga. But she had to get her whole idea into her poem, about the heroes being made out of Denmark, and about the monument, and about the heroes who had returned to the soil again. It was a very important idea, almost the same as Pastor Gregersen put into his funeral sermons. "Earth thou art and to earth returneth." That was, after all, the same notion, and it came right out of the Bible. There were things about war and peace in the Bible, too, she knew. She remembered one of Pastor Gregersen's prayers at the monument on Liberation Day. So the idea wasn't Fru Fugl's, really, and not the idea of the scientist who wrote the textbook, either. It was nobody's idea except somebody long ago who wrote the Bible or got it straight from God.

She felt shaken when she thought of that. She ought to put that in a poem. Not this poem, but a special poem, maybe. Peace. War. She was chewing her pencil so hard that she felt bits of wood in her mouth and tasted lead. It seemed to her that the taste of poem-writing was the taste of lead. Farmor got cross when she found the pencils all chewed up, but not nearly so cross as when she saw Lotte's fingernails chewed clear to the quick, with sore corners. "I'm going to put soap on your fingers to keep them out of your mouth," she had said, and once she made Lotte wear gloves to read.

Peace. War. Denmark is a land of peace—*ja*, it was coming. "Denmark is a land of peace, but sometimes there is war—" *War* would be a good rhyme. Then "Far" could come in,

"And many houses through the land
Have not any Far . . ."

That was a very bad rhythm, that last line—and not long enough, either. Maybe "are without a Far." But it wasn't as good a stanza as the other two, and it ought to be better. In a poem each stanza should get better up to a fine, strong one at the end. She must work on this one. She sighed and worked and worked. Maybe she should get the Big Idea written down and come back to this one. Sometimes the rhymes and rhythms came all of a sudden, almost by themselves. "Then great Danish stones are found like those of ancient days," she wrote carefully, "and stand beside the roadsides, telling where—" Excited, she saw that it had happened; she had actually found her rhyme along with the idea. "Where the heroes *are*." She looked back at the peace and war stanza.

"Then Danish stones along the roads
Tell who the heroes are,
And country homes and city homes
Lack brother, Farfar, Far—"

That put the idea into one stanza instead of taking two! She read it over. The last line didn't sound right at all. But she could think about it. Sometimes when she just tucked a poor verse into the back of her mind, she suddenly had it right and it was wonderful, as if it had written itself. A person's thoughts just sort of went on and on and on when you were doing other things, maybe washing or studying or doing dishes or walking or riding your bicycle. It was nice when that happened, a kind of miracle. Of course, it didn't happen very often, it was terribly special. As special as a best friend. There weren't many of those, the kind you talked to even when you weren't talking, like Lisa sometimes. Not all the time but lots of times. Suddenly she thought of going to America and not having any friend she could talk to without talking. The poem vanished from her mind, idea, rhythm, and all. Imagine—no Lisa. Nobody to *tell*. Of course, there would be Mor, over there. But at school—and all talking English, nobody at all talking Danish. There were things you could tell your best friend that you couldn't even tell your Mor, or Farmor, or anybody. Lisa-things.

It was odd how you liked people in different ways, and needed them in different ways too. . . . And then, as if the magic were working in spite of everything, she got an idea for the poem out of that idea about Lisa and friends. About Liberation Day.

> "Danish children march together
> On Liberation Day,"

she wrote, and paused, and tasted lead for the length of a long and serious thought. Then she wrote slowly:

> "They put bright flags and flowers on
> The monument of gray . . ."

Maybe it would be better to say "monuments" because most monuments were gray, and there were monuments all over Denmark, not only here in Jutland at their own crossroads. Children would be marching all over Denmark. All over, north and south and east and west. And for the last part—

The lead broke right in two, and she had to peel off the soft wood to make another length for writing. She began going once more through the alphabet. Bay. Cay—no such word—day, she had used that already. . . . Fay. Gay was a good word, but you couldn't put a word like gay in a sad stanza about gravestones. Yet—if she could use "gay," it would make "gray" seem even grayer. And sadder. The fars and brothers and husbands were gay before they were dead. Even when they were being heroes, out in the dark night, they made jokes together, as Ole said. Hr. Axel had written about how they never lost their good humor, even when they were to be shot. That was hard to believe, but he said they were brave enough to keep their spirits up in spite of being afraid. Suddenly she had it:

> "And read the names they know so well
> Of Fars who were so gay."

Oh, it *was* sad! Tears sprang to her eyes. She read the whole stanza aloud, all six lines slowly and thoughtfully, and before she finished, tears were running down her cheeks. Far had been gay; Mor always told about how gay he was. And she could remember, just a little, being swung up onto his shoulder—and looking down into laughter. People all told how gay Ole's grandfather had been and how Ole inherited his sense of humor. But now all the gay ones lay under the gray stones.

Now—she blew her nose. Now it was almost finished. Nothing more need be said except about peace. She wanted to end it with something about how the heroes had brought peace to Denmark.

> "Now instead of deadly planes
> The lark's far, flying high—"

Nej, "flies up high—"

> "Now, instead of deadly planes
> The lark is flying high,
> Sending songs down to the nest
> Where wife and babies lie—"

That was very good but not an ending for the idea, yet. She chewed hard and got up and stared out of the window, thinking about larks. Of course, there were no larks yet. The sky had looked gray and sad yesterday, just right for such a poem. But soon, surely before the Fifth of May, sunshine would fill the sky and flood over the world, and everything in the ground would begin to grow. Things grew faster in Denmark than anywhere because the sun shone both night and day during the growing time.

How to end it? She began on the alphabet once more. By. Maybe. Cy—cry—*sky!* She tried that for a while, but it was not right. Die. It was strong and good and would make the larks even sadder, as *gay* did for *gray.*

But the idea. And then it came, not exactly right yet, but the idea was right. And yes, it was an ending.

> "And children march together
> Who may grow up and *not die.*"

That was the idea of peace at the end instead of war. And the good sadness was there, but the words were wrong. She tried again:

> "They laugh and march and sing together,
> Remembering—"

And again—

> "The Danish children march together,
> And like the lark, they sing
> How lovely Denmark is, and how
> They are remembering
> Danish heroes—"

Nej— "the Holger Danske—who died—as heroes—"
That line was too long, but she hurried on, for suddenly she knew she was on the trail of the right way. *Spring.* The lark sang in spring, and Liberation Day was in spring, and being a child was spring. And things that had died were growing. *Ja.* Excited, she began working on the final line.

"So peace—" Peace and spring. "So peace could come in spring . . ." It was not right yet, as if she had got *spring* only to make a rhyme, in spite of the lark and everything. But after a moment she wrote slowly, "For peace another spring . . ." *Ja, ja, ja!* Excited, she wrote the final lines,

> ". . . remembering
> The Holger Danske who died to bring
> Peace another spring."

Now of all things, she suddenly saw that she had four rhymes instead of only three. They had just happened. It did not matter, it was even wonderful because it made the final stanza better than all the others.

She could not sleep until she had taken the final copy

downstairs. Her heart pounded as she said, "Farmor—here is a poem for the contest. I've just finished it."

It was almost unbearable to be in the same room while Farmor read. Lotte bit a nail, and Farmor looked up and said, "Now, Lotte—" And read again. Then she got up and came over and leaned down and put a kiss square on Lotte's mouth.

"It's beautiful," she said. And there were tears in her eyes!

"Do you think it'll win the prize?" Lotte asked.

Farmor stood up straight. "If *I* were the judge—" she said. "But then—Lotte, it seems wonderful to me. And I can't imagine who has a child who could do better. But then, if I were a judge, you would get first prize for everything—"

Lotte went upstairs again, walking in time to the poem as if there were music in the air. What if somebody should set it to music? And people sang it like "Denmark Is a Lovely Land."

Mor would hear it on the radio, far off in New York. "Lotte? Lotte wrote that?" she would cry. "Pat—the King has made Lotte poet laureate of Denmark! It was on the news today. So of course—she can't possibly leave Denmark now—how could the poet laureate leave Denmark, ever again?"

CHAPTER TEN

❊

Living Light

"What are you going to wear today?" Lisa's voice came, excited, over the telephone.

"I haven't thought about it. What are you?"

"My white American dress," Lisa said.

She had received three American dresses exactly like Lotte's, only different colors. "I thought maybe both of us—today—you could be red and I white, almost like a Danish flag—"

Lotte did not want to wear one of her American dresses for Liberation Day, even though they were the prettiest dresses she had. "We don't need to dress alike *every* day," she said, her voice cold.

"But this *isn't* just *every* day!" Lisa cried. And of course it wasn't; it was the Fifth of May, the day they had been waiting for, for weeks and weeks. For a minute, Lotte felt stubborn; she went hard inside in a queer way that was getting familiar. It made her a little sick when it happened, and she was always sorry afterward; but lately Lisa had been quite bothersome, bragging all the time about how special her essay was. She seemed absolutely certain she was going to win. And when she said, "I've never been to Copenhagen, Lotte—everybody else has been there, you dozens of times, and Ole went last summer—and imagine—if I win, I can go when you get on your ship, and we could go to Tivoli together, couldn't we, and see the Royal Guard *together*—"

Then Lotte had a bad feeling. Guilty. The second prize was a set of books—and she would rather have them, really, because, of course, she was going to Copenhagen anyhow, as Lisa said. But if she won first prize, she thought, she could take the books (if Lisa got second prize) and give the trip to Lisa. People would say, "Isn't it nice of Lotte to give Lisa that wonderful trip!"

Thinking of this and of the Two Pleasures besides, she decided to wear the dress Lisa wanted her to wear, after all. "All right, I'll wear the red one," she said. Immediately she felt happy. Why didn't she remember that when she made Lisa happy, she herself felt happier right away? As she got onto her bicycle, she looked up at the blue, blue sky in a kind of marveling gladness. Spring! How lovely spring was in Denmark! It was because winter was so long here, as people said, and so dark. People came out of their heavy clothes as soon as the sun brought the first spring flowers bursting from the ground under the trees. From fur overcoats into bathing suits. That was Denmark. And everything began to grow, night and day, for the sun stayed longer and longer until, in June, it shone all day and most of the night as well.

"Well—now you can go outside and play," Farmor had said. "You won't miss your mother so much—" Of course, that wasn't true. The truth was that there were outside things that reminded Lotte of Mor as well as inside things. The space Mor left behind was huge, in or out, which seemed strange, since she herself was so little. Her absence was a constant pain, even in the middle of the goodness of spring.

There came the mailman, pedaling along in his bright red coat. He stopped Lotte and said, "Want your mail?" Every single day, ever since Mor and Patrick had gone, there was mail for Lottegaard. Postcards or letters or packages— something every single day.

"Two cards for your book today," the mailman said. He had been very interested in the book Patrick sent for her to put postcards in. It had transparent plastic pages, and the cards went between so that you could read the card and look at the pictures too. Today it was a high building, and she knew the postman was interested, so she read what Patrick had written: "Here is our apartment house. That man in front is the doorman; he dresses in his fancy suit every day, gold buttons and all. He's almost as handsome as the King's guards, isn't he? You'll like him—and he'd better like you, because nobody can come in or out unless he says so." On the picture Patrick had drawn a line from the street to the top—and by a little balcony he had written: "This is Us!"

"You go up and down on an elevator?" asked the mail-man.

"*Ja*—so high you look down at birds," she said.

"Isn't that wonderful?" the postman said. "You'll go home on an elevator, instead of down a lane!"

Imagine, she thought.

"It's getting close now, isn't it?" The postman smiled as he spoke, as if he thought she was pleased. "I hope you're mark-ing your calendar, just like Hr. Patrick said—" He had seen the fine calendar Patrick sent, on each page a colored picture of something in America. The Grand Canyon, Niagara Falls, old houses in New Orleans, the Rocky Mountains, Seal Rocks in San Francisco, the Empire State Building. Patrick had put golden stars on all special American days— the Fourth of July, Thanksgiving, Christmas, Veterans' Day, (which was rather like Liberation Day, celebrated with flags, though, and not with candles, Patrick said), Flag Day, Washington's Birthday and Lincoln's Birthday and Jefferson's Birthday, and St. Valentine's Day. And her birthday. And he had put a whole circle of gold stars on June 26, with a tiny snapshot of the *Oslofjord,* because that was her sailing day. "Your Mor has a calendar just like this one," he had written, "and she has put red stars on all the great Danish Days, and every night, just before bedtime, she runs a line through the date and says, 'Now—one day less before Lotte comes!' "

So Lotte had marked all the Danish days too. On the Fifth of May she had drawn a little Danish flag, for May Day a Maypole, and for Midsummer Day a witch burning over a bright orange fire.

The postman went off down the lane, and Lotte pedaled on, feeling the warm spring breeze under her skirts. It was going to be a wonderful day for the parade, with such a sky and only a few flying clouds. Lisa stood waiting at the crossroads. She had two small flags, pins her Mor had given her. "Lotte—look—Mor says we're to wear these over our hearts—"

They pinned them on each other, and Lotte had to agree that to wear white and red had been a fine idea. She would tell Mor about it, and Mor would be glad she had sent the right colors. But what color had she not sent? She wrote that she had never seen such wonderful clothes as in America, and for so little money. "Today," she had written, "I went through *hundreds* of dresses in a shop on our street. They had a two-for-the-price-of-one sale. Imagine that! So I got two of each one, thinking what fun it would be for you and Lisa to dress alike now and then."

"Let's take a picnic tomorrow," Lisa said, as they rode on toward school. And then she laughed and said, "Imagine, Lotte—*tomorrow we will know who won—*"

We'll know today, Lotte thought, and looked at her watch. In two hours and thirty-two minutes, they would know.

"We can go to the woods tomorrow," Lisa said. "I asked Mor, and she said I could go if I'd take Per—I've got to tend him while she goes to town. Do you mind if he goes?"

"Of course not." Lotte looked at the trees on the brow of almost every hill. Never had spring been lovelier, she thought. The beechwoods were now the tender color of unfolding leaves, and she thought of what Mor once said about beechwoods, as they lay looking up after a picnic: "A beech tree is a living cathedral." That would make a fine poem. The trees were tall spires, and the bright sun through the leaves was like colored windows throwing designs on the grass.

"Are you nervous today, too?" Lisa asked. "Mor said I couldn't wipe the dishes this morning—I was so shaky and excited I dropped a glass." As they walked into the building, she took Lotte's hand. "I'd be almost as glad if *you* won," she said. "But, Lotte—we could have such fun if I got to go to Copenhagen!"

Lotte said nothing. The night before she had prayed to win, and when Farmor came to kiss her goodnight, she had asked, "Farmor, do you think I'll win? Do you?" And Farmor had said the same old thing. "I'm not the judge, Lotte. And it seems to me the important thing isn't winning, anyway, but having had such a lovely idea and having written such a fine poem."

She knew Farmor wouldn't like her to pray to win. Once, when she was littler, she had asked, aloud, for God to send her some new skates. "I will do my lessons tomorrow if You send me some new skates." Farmor and Mor had both scolded her. "It's as if you were trying to make a *bargain* with God," Mor had said, looking shocked. But it seemed to Lotte that one made bargains with God all the time. Even the Pastor sometimes said that the people would be good if God sent them blessings—she had heard him.

The school was noisy today, but Fru Fugl was so excited herself she didn't seem to care. She announced that they might read whatever they liked until time to go to the auditorium. "Our friends and relations will begin coming at ten," she said. "I am expecting Hr. Axel a little before that."

Ole raised his hand. "Has he already told you the winner?" he asked.

Fru Fugl shook her head. "I asked him to make me wait along with everybody else," she said. "It was hard—but I did! I told him I liked every essay in this class so much that I was glad to leave the judging to him. I never could have given only three prizes—"

She asked Ole and some of the other boys to distribute the flags. Every child was to carry one into the auditorium and in the parade. How beautiful it would look as they waved them in time to the music of the band!

"Now—quiet! No laughing, please, as we march in— Karen! Face front, please. Bo—Eric! No whispering. No laughing—now—march!"

Each class was to take a certain place, with the band marching into the auditorium first, playing "King Christian." Fru Fugl marched to their place with the class and then, with a smile, she rushed back up the aisle. To meet Hr. Axel, of course. People greeted her as she hurried by. It was a wonderful day for her, Lotte thought. And for some others too—but who, only Hr. Axel knew.

"There they are—" Lisa whispered. And sure enough, Hr. Axel and Fru Fugl appeared through a curtain at the back of the stage. Hr. Axel had a leather folder in his hands. Then came Hr. Gustavsen, the janitor, with a small table, which he set beside the reading stand. He disappeared and came back with a box—that would be the prize set of books, perhaps. And on top of it he set a single book. The third prize, a history of Denmark, illustrated, with the name of the winner stamped in gold . . .

People were watching, sitting quietly under the pleasant thunder of the band, while Fru Fugl came forward and stood waiting. When the final notes came and the band stopped with a ruffle of drums, there was a sudden quiet. Lotte heard the steady thudding of her own heart.

Fru Fugl greeted everybody, but neither Lotte or Lisa really heard what she was saying. Hr. Axel was taking papers from his folder— "And we know you are all anxious to know the results . . . so there will be no delay. . . . Hr.

Axel—" People were clapping hard as he stood up, and he smiled like an actor or somebody on television. "I have never in my life had so hard a task," he said. "Fru Fugl knew she could not decide which of her fine students did the best work, and so she made *me* do it instead." There was a gentle laugh, quickly hushed. "I kept wishing I had thirty prizes instead of only three—and at one point I felt like telephoning Fru Fugl and saying, 'Why don't we just give the prize to the whole class and take them all on an excursion to Tivoli?' Would you like that?" He seemed to be asking the whole class, and they began to clap.

"Wouldn't that be wonderful?" Lisa whispered, and Lotte saw that Fru Fugl was beaming until her face was quite red. Now the people of the neighborhood would know just how good her idea had been.

"But she said I must make a decision," Hr. Axel said, "and so I did. I tried to be as fair as I could, marking each paper on three things, one by one. The correctness of form—whether the grammar and spelling and writing were all exactly right. Of course, Fru Fugl had seen to that so carefully that I found hardly a mistake in the lot! Then the style—how clearly and how beautifully the writer had expressed himself. This is much harder than grammar, as every writer knows. And then—this was most important of all—I tried to judge which of the pieces had the most original idea."

He picked up a paper. It was all but unbearable the way Lotte's heart was beating. She glanced at Lisa and saw her eyes looking glazed and set from staring at Hr. Axel, her hands not folded now, but clenched—

"I am going to ask each winning author to come forward and read his own work," Hr. Axel said. First, the winner of the third prize—" He turned and picked up the big book on the table. "This is a volume of Danish history, illustrated with great paintings. The name of this winner is stamped on the cover in gold." He blinked at the book through his glasses, and there was hardly a sound in the whole auditorium as the people waited. He had to tease just a little; it was his Danish way. "It is hard to read that shining new gold," he said, "but I think—it—says—"

Not this time, Lotte thought.

But it was. It was her own name. She saw the turning of eyes as he said it—she sat under the eyes of the whole crowd, and they were clapping, stretching to see, and she felt Lisa's hand come out and close on hers.

"If Lotte will come forward," Hr. Axel said, and he was smiling as if she should be the happiest person in the world. She felt herself rise and move to the end of the aisle and hoped, desperately, that her legs would not fail her before she got to the stage and up the steps. *Only third!* How she could read her poem with her throat as tight as that, she did not know. It was all unreal, and yet there was Hr. Axel's hand shaking hers, and then she felt the weight of the big book and saw her name on it. A flashbulb made a sudden light. "Well, thank goodness we are not lost today!" Hr. Axel said, and everybody laughed, remembering the picture in the newspaper. "Lotte, it was very hard not to give you the first prize because you have written a most beautiful poem for Denmark. In form and style you were 100 per cent, higher than anybody. But I did not think your idea was

your own, though it is beautiful and it is true. Now let our
friends hear your poem." He handed her the familiar paper
on which she had worked so long to make the penmanship
quite perfect, and he sat down beside Fru Fugl, and Lotte
stood alone. Hr. Gustavsen came out and lowered the microphone, so it stood just in front of her.

"My Motherland." She had not been certain that her voice would come, but it did. It seemed to stand before her in the air because of the microphone. But it went into the waiting of the whole room of people, and she thought suddenly of Farmor down there with Tove and everybody—all of her old friends—

> "They say that I am Motherland
> And Motherland is me.
> When I was young, I wondered
> However that could be . . ."

She heard a little ripple of laughter when she read "when I was young . . ." and she lifted her chin and stiffened her back. "But now I understand . . ."

Verse after verse, she read each one more firmly than the last. When she came to the Holger Danske, she felt as if she were ringing a bell with the words, they came out so proudly:

> ". . . remembering
> The Holger Danske who died to bring
> Peace another spring!"

The clapping was like standing on the edge of the sea. She felt Fru Fugl's hand taking hers—she was weeping!— and Hr. Axel's once more, and the band began to play "Denmark Is a Lovely Land" as she went down the steps and back to her place through the clapping on either side.

Lisa was waiting. She took Lotte's hand the moment she sat down, and as Hr. Axel stood up again, with another paper and the clapping died away, she clung to it. She was still waiting, Lotte knew, and still hoping.

"You will think I am partial to poetry," Hr. Axel said, "and perhaps I am, in a way, for it is the most difficult form of all. This poem, to which I have given second prize—this set of books, an encyclopedia—is not rhymed at all but is in the great tradition of much classical poetry, in a loose ten-beat line. Listen—

"'On May the fourth in 1945,
   At eight and 37 by the clock,
   Came the happy voice of B.B.C.
   Victory is ours! Repeat—repeat—
   Victory is ours! and peace—and peace!'"

Lotte felt the strength of the words as he read them. *Ja,* it was a good poem, even without any rhymes. She could hear that. And there went Ole as his name was pronounced, his grin as wide as his face. On the stand he read in a loud, firm voice as if he had no fear at all. It was a very long poem, pages and pages, but nobody in the whole auditorium made a sound as he read.

"Down came the blackout curtains from the windows,
   On went the lights on every avenue,
   Up went the flags and fluttered in the wind,
   As bands marched proudly through the thronging streets.
   And then a candle stood bright in one window—
   Another one! Another one! Until
   Every window in the city glowed
   With living light—"

Ja, Lotte thought, it was better than hers, after all. She had a strange squeeze of pain to think it, but there it was.

And now what? What in the world could be even better? She glanced at Lisa—surely not Lisa. Ole came down, laughing and carrying the whole set of books, lugging it alone until one of his friends leaped up to help. "I want my prize right now!" Ole said. The room was alive with good laughter and noise, and once more the band played. And once more the hush.

"Now for the first prize," Hr. Axel said and held up another sheaf of papers. Lotte felt Lisa's hand, hot and wet in hers. The whole auditorium seemed suddenly very hot. "This one has the prize, although it hadn't the best form—it was not as high in some things as the other two you have heard, even as some of those not given prizes at all. But it had the best idea of all, in my opinion—THE FRIENDS OF PEACE."

Lotte felt Lisa's hand go limp, and then met her eyes. *Ja, ja,* it was Lisa's. "It begins," Hr. Axel said, "with a quotation from General Eisenhower, who was so beloved of all of us during the troubled days of the occupation. It is from an article he called 'An Epidemic of Friendship'—an article that he wrote about Scandinavians and our great program 'Meet the Danes' and Sweden's 'Sweden at Home' and Norway's 'Know the Norwegians' and Finland's 'Find the Finns' and a worldwide organization that is being made of all the different nations who long for peace and want to know each other, not as political beings or business people but just as people longing for peace. General Eisenhower has said—" Hr. Axel looked up. "But let the author read it to you from beginning to end," he said. "Lisa—!" The burst of clapping came so swiftly that one could not even hear

Lisa's last name. For a second, as she stood up and Lotte felt her hand move away, Lotte had that old flash of envy, like pain. But it did not last. Lisa's glad face was as wonderful as the lovely little skip she made as she moved up the aisle. Now she can go to Copenhagen with me! Lotte thought. And she thought of the Two Pleasures, and this one—*ja*—this one was better than her own, better than she would have felt for herself, she knew it. Lisa's pretty voice came out over the audience, almost too pretty and light for the serious subject of her essay. "We hear too—" She read very well, better as she came toward the end: "We hear too much about war, as President Eisenhower has said, and too little about peace. Yet war brings nothing but suffering and misery and the anxiety of people all over the world. Our friendship in time of war is apparent to everybody because it brings soldiers and guns and ships to allies. But in times of peace who hears about the gifts from land to land? Our newspapers were full of appreciation for the gifts of pilots who flew over Denmark during the war, like our American friend Patrick, who says he loved Denmark before he ever stood upon her soil. But we should think even more about the gift America gave us almost fifty years ago, Rebild Park and its Lincoln Cabin and the flagstaff, where Danish and American flags flew together even during the war. Now, every year, thousands of Americans come here to celebrate American Independence Day, the Fourth of July. This is a wonderful thing, and we wonder why more and more countries cannot celebrate Independence Days for and with each other. Every country has some great day that we might put on our World Calendars and remember. Maybe the People to People organization can fix this for us—a calendar of the celebrations of the whole world. On our own Liberation Day, let us keep this thought in our hearts, for peace in Denmark is not enough. We must find a way to have peace in the whole world."

Lisa stood bowing. Fru Fugl rose and kissed her. Hr. Axel shook her hand and gave her an envelope. "This is an envelope full of tickets," he said. "They will take you to Copenhagen and back again, by bus, train, and ferry. They will take you to Tivoli for a whole day, with a ride on everything and meals in any restaurant you choose. They will take you, free, into any museum in the city, and for a tour through the publication and printing offices of my paper, *Politiken*."

A sigh went through the whole great listening crowd. Tivoli—Copenhagen—the ferry!

And then Hr. Axel said: "Your teacher, Fru Fugl, has an announcement to make—about a prize for every single one who submitted anything to this competition. The publishers of *Politiken* were so impressed that they want to publish every single one of the entries, prize ones and all. And they would like to sponsor a Class Day—an excursion."

Excursions were not unheard of, of course, but such a one, clear to Copenhagen, sponsored and arranged by the great newspaper in Copenhagen! For a few moments, it was as if the whole auditorium sat stunned. And then pandemonium! The children began to clap, and then the band began to play. When Lisa came from the stage between Hr. Axel and Fru Fugl, marching proudly down the aisle, everybody followed, the band playing the whole time as hard as it could play. And with flying flags they marched down the road in the bright sun.

"Let me help you light the candles," Hr. Axel said to Lotte that evening. "Remember when I was here before?"

Of course she remembered. Mor had been here too, then. She said, "It will be fun to have you help—" and thought, Why can't people just *stay?* Everything was nice in a place, and then people began to go away, one by one.

As dusk fell, they moved together from room to room, last of all, the Lotte Room, as always. When they came in, the hangings on the old bed looked mysterious and shadowy. To think of all the Lottes who had slept there and had gone away! Lotte felt a stir at the roots of her hair. Maybe they had died there, some of them, in that very bed. But she did not want to ask Farmor such a thing or think of it. Her hand trembled as she lighted the last candle, and she thought how the hands of the first Lotte must have opened and closed these very windows many times, perhaps set candles here too. Not for Liberation Day, for there was no such celebration then, but for Christmas surely. And there had been no electricity then. Lotte the First had read by candlelight.

"Look," Farmor said. "You can see candles burning all down the road."

In every house they were to be seen now, for from this window one saw the whole grand sweep of the countryside. The grand old man had chosen a wonderful place to build his house.

As they stood looking out, an airplane flew across the sky.

Many flew by, every day, but just now, tonight, this one seemed very special. The heroes, Lotte thought, had flown over—her Far. And Patrick, as Lisa had said. She felt herself reaching across the sky, across the land and across the water, wondering whether Mor might light a candle in the high windows of her New York house tonight. How strange—if she did, it might be the only candle in thousands of windows there.

"Let's go outside and see how it looks," she said. They always did that. And always they went out to see how the Christmas tree looked from the gate. An Inside Pleasure and an Outside Pleasure—two other Pleasures, Lotte thought, and when she stood at the gate and saw the candles burning in every window of Lottegaard, she knew she had never seen anything more beautiful and never would. Softly the lights glowed through the dusk, yellow and wavering and alive.

"Somebody has put candles in the church," Farmor said. "In the tower—look—"

"And on the monument," Hr. Axel said.

Lotte thought of the heroes, as Fru Fugl said they ought to do. Of Farfar and of Far. She remembered Farmor telling how Far's airplane had come in the night, skimming the dark heath, so close to his old home that he could have landed in the meadow if only he were able to land at all.

"Lotte, we'll always think of you when we light the candles in Denmark," Hr. Axel said, "and we hope you'll think of us and light a candle over there in America." It was as if he had read her mind. "You'll be doing as Lisa said in her essay—taking something of Denmark to America with you.

I read once about the emigrants going there—how they all took with them their 'invisible baggage,' all their ways of doing and their love for their old homes. That's what has made America such a great country—it is all countries in one, the way no other country in the whole world has ever been. Did you ever think about that? *You'll be carrying over there your Danish candle—*"

CHAPTER ELEVEN

Birthday

Now there was no need to count the days. The whole class counted them and especially Lisa. One would have thought she counted the hours, for she talked of little else but "when we are in Copenhagen . . ." She looked at pictures she had seen all her life, but with new eyes now that she herself would see such places for sure, on a Certain Day.

On Liberation Day there were fifty-one more days until June 26 and forty-five until the twentieth of June, which was the last day of school. Lotte marked her calendar every morning, but not as Lisa did. Lisa's heart was high, and when Lotte thought of Mor, of seeing Mor anywhere, hers had a skip of its own. But always, just underneath—and never mentioned—was the heavy dread.

The first day she and Lisa climbed into the tree house and hauled up water and soap and rags to clean it, she could not help saying, "Lisa, sometimes I think you forget *I won't be here—after—*"

Lisa did not look at her. She began to scrub hard at the smudges on the little window. "I *try* to forget," she said. And when the cleaning was finished, and they shook and put down their little rag rug and hung curtains that Ida had washed and starched, she said, "I won't come here any more when you're gone, even if—"

"Farmor will want you to."

"She told me she would. She said I could bring Per or any-body."

Then she talked of writing there and in two minutes was laughing again. "Just because you are going to die for sure," she said one day as they sat together with their lessons in the little house, "you don't talk about dying every day."

Why think of sad things, anyway, now that the meadows stretched green in every direction. How marvelous it was to see the grass springing and the buds appearing on the trees and bushes and then, suddenly, as if overnight, roses bloomed along the fences and lilacs made every lane a paradise. Birds woke Lotte each morning, whole choruses of them, and there was, one day, miraculously, a father stork standing on top of the house, and his mate came, and soon she sat quietly on what looked like a pile of sticks he had fetched for her. Two families of ducks swam on the pond, which was blue with sky-reflections, and three tiny cygnets followed Far-mor's swans, each making its own tiny wake on the water. In the barn new families of *lillegrise* suckled in pink heaps, and there were three calves and a wild funny colt, who ran in the meadow behind the house and soon learned to nuzzle into a pocket for a sugar lump.

Finn brought vegetables from his garden, proud of the first small sweet radishes and tiny onions and delicate let-tuce. One day he brought the first strawberries, and then Lotte and Lisa knew it was possible to find wild ones as well along the road.

Day by day, the days were marked by Nature herself; Lotte hardly needed to put the crosses on her calendar. "And that is the end of May. Now it is this month—" The day before her birthday, she saw the first tourists after school, coming from the inn.

Lisa said, "We'll have to get our Number Notebooks out." Every year they played the game along with all the other children who lived near highways and inns and ferryboats, taking license numbers. It was fun to compare them. Who had gotten the most today? From the farthest away? In the fall there would be a huge count to discover who had gotten the most and the farthest for the whole summer. "Do you imagine they take license numbers in America?" She could not imagine standing on Fifth Avenue taking numbers. There would be too many cars altogether. Even Patrick said there was too much and too many of everything in America.

Lisa was to come to dinner on Lotte's birthday, and she was going to stay all night. Farmor said, soon after Liberation Day, "I hope you don't mind not having a party this year, Lotte. When your mother was here, I felt we could manage, but this year—" And she added, "This year, there will be plenty of parties at school—and Lisa is having a good-by party—"

Party or no, there were plenty of birthday secrets at Lottegaard. That always happened, just as it did before Christmas. She saw Farmor and Ida whispering, saw a huge mysterious package arrive and disappear without being opened.

Mor wrote, "Today Pat and I walked in Central Park and saw the children's zoo and H. C. Andersen sitting with his book. There is a charming little bronze duck beside him that children can sit on. It seems wonderful to me that children over here love him as we do."

Two days before Lotte's birthday, Farmor and Ida and

two other girls, who came especially to help, gave Lotte-gaard its spring cleaning from cellar to roof. They washed everything and took down the curtains and put the rugs out to be beaten on the grass. Pictures were taken down and cleaned and hung again. Even the thatch was mended, so that bright yellow spots of new straw stood out on the old dark brown around the chimneys. Lotte helped dust the books while Ida washed the shelves. She took a long time about it, because every book was so interesting she kept forgetting to dust and just read and looked at pictures. "If you stop for every one," Ida said, "we'll never finish."

But the books were mostly about Denmark, as the paintings on the wall were, and Lotte loved every one. Farfar had loved the sea as well as the woods and fields, even though he was a farmer. "Sometimes he wished he could leave the land and sail around the world," Farmor said. "But as soon as we set sail, even on a ferryboat, he began to long for ground under his feet again."

There were books by all the great Danish writers—Johannes Ewald, and Oehlenschläger and Sören Kierkegaard and Georg Brandes, and J. P. Jacobsen and Johannes V. Jensen and Karin Michaelis who called herself "The Little Troll," and, of course, lots and lots of H. C. Andersen. There were the plays of Kaj Munk, who had been shot by the Germans for his powerful writings and lay in an honored grave in Jutland. Steen Steensen Blicher, the great poet called the Heath Lark, had lived right in this neighborhood, and Lotte knew many of his poems by heart. One of Farmor's paintings showed him on the heath talking to the gypsies, and one of them showed H. C. Andersen reading his stories to a little sick girl. Farmor had so many pictures that two whole walls of the living room were covered with them, and every other wall in the house held a share. Patrick had thought it wonderful, all the books and pictures people had in Denmark. "Even farmers!" he had said.

"But farmers have a great deal of time to read," Farmor had said, surprised. "Especially in the wintertime. What do they do in America if they have no books?"

And Patrick had said, "I am beginning to wonder—"

It seemed a shame, when one was not having a party, for a birthday to fall on Sunday. But from the moment Lotte opened her eyes, it was made Her Special Day. Farmor woke her. "Lotte—the sun is coming up, and Finn is raising your flag. You must go to the window."

There he was, drawing the ropes, and the bright red and white banner whipped in the wind. Everybody in the neighborhood would see it and know it was a festival day at Lotte-gaard.

Breakfast was pancakes. Dinner would be chicken and strawberries. One had all the favorite things on one's own day. "You may open one of your boxes at breakfast," Farmor said. "The rest can wait for Lisa to see—" They all stood around while she untied the ribbons. It was a huge box—and she knew before taking the white tissue paper away that it was more American clothes. "To make you beautiful on your Day," Mor had written on her card, "and for once, don't forget your gloves for church." The dress was blue, fluffy and summery, with a full petticoat to make the skirt stand out. And there was a white cape trimmed with blue and a hat and gloves and purse to go with it. In the purse was a gay handkerchief and a tiny bottle of perfume. Just like Mor—all of it.

When Lotte went upstairs to get ready for church, she suddenly got a familiar old feeling—stubbornness, like a lump of lead in her stomach. Carefully, she put on one of her ordinary old Sunday dresses and took out an old purse and gloves. She knew just how dismayed Farmor would look when she came down the stairs.

"Lotte, your mother wanted you to wear—"

"How can she know what I wear?" Lotte asked.

"Because—" Farmor came to her and took her hands and looked at her, hard. "I am to take your picture today, did you know that? It's all arranged. We are taking flowers for the Lottes, the way we always have. And your mother will know *because I will tell her*—"

She turned Lotte firmly around. "Now let the birthday storm be over," she said, "and let the sun come out."

Farmor and Ida had made a wreath for each of the Lotte graves, lilacs and roses from the garden and beside the road and from the meadows red poppies and white ox-eye daisies. They went early to the church and walked around to the row of stones. On the oldest of all, Farmor hung a wreath so that the worn words could be read in a circle of flowers:

Her Hviler Vor Elskede Husfru Og Moder
LOTTE RASMUSSEN KNUDSEN
Født 1756-1825

"Here rests our beloved Wife and Mother."

Lotte had never before minded standing beside those old

graves. But today her heart beat slowly and thickly, as if it were bathed in glue. If only her birthday had been on a schoolday this year so she could have spent it all with Lisa and her friends, so she might have served cake and punch as she had the last year. She did not want to think of old sad things on this birthday because she was too sad already. If only she might walk in the bright sunshine or ride her bicycle and just think of strawberries and cake. And laugh. But she must go into the church instead, with Farmor, and listen to the creaking old organ and feel the cold stone through her shoes. Even at midsummer the church was never really warm, as if winter had got into the ancient stones and could never be got out again. But of course she loved it—even today, not wanting to go in at all, she knew she would remember it with love. It was a pretty white church with a steep tower and high, colored windows. Over the altar was a picture she had always liked of Jesus preaching to the wise men when He was a little boy. Great vases of roses and lilacs stood on the altar today, which was covered with a lace cloth. Tall white candles burned in golden candlesticks. Along the edges of the high arches were red and white stripes, which had been painted many years ago and looked very gay, and there was a lovely little ship model hanging from the roof, with its sails all spread to an imaginary wind. It had been given to the church many years ago by a family whose son had been lost at sea. Here every Lotte had been christened and confirmed and married and buried. Every Lotte had told time by that same old clock in the tower and had listened to the same organ and to the same old bell. And to many long sermons, Lotte thought with a sigh. She saw Lisa come with her whole benchful of family and Ole with his.

She was glad when the service was over and she and Farmor started out. She wanted to catch Lisa— But the Pastor stopped her with a kindly arm around her shoulders. "We are going to miss you, Lotte," he said. "When my father was pastor here, he used to be asked to bless those emigrating to America. I am seldom asked to do it now, but lately—I was telling my wife this morning—lately I have blessed my own emigrants."

An *emigrant*. How odd it sounded, as if she were somebody in a history book! But Hr. Axel had spoken of it too, and of her "invisible baggage."

"You are lucky you won't have to sail on a small ship for six months to get there as they did a hundred years ago!" Fru Gregersen said.

Lotte stood listening politely while they talked of other things, tugging just a little at Farmor's sleeve. But of course Lisa would wait. And *ja,* there she was. "I told Finn we would walk home today," Farmor said. "Such a lovely day!"

And it was fun; they skipped ahead and made circles around Farmor who walked slowly, smiling at them and stopping to pick mint for her tea. "Having you is better than a party," Lotte said. "I didn't even *want* a party. Farmor says we can take some cake and strawberries and things later and have tea in the little house."

Lisa's face was as red as could be, and as they went up the walk, Lotte knew something was queer. Lisa could never keep a secret from her face. Before she turned the handle of the door and opened it, she knew what was waiting.

Children were coming down the stairway, through every door, crowding the hall, and every one of them, with Fru Fugl in the middle, was shouting and pelting her with flowers. "Surprise! Surprise! Happy birthday! *Tillykke, tillykke!*"

Mor had planned it all with Fru Fugl. There were funny hats for everybody and confetti and serpentines and bags of streamers to throw at each other the way people did on New Year's Eve. And in the dining room the table was bright with flowers and flags, and a huge birthday cake sat in the center. There were too many to sit down, so they all filed by for napkins and sandwiches and salad and potato chips, and then all went out onto the lawn to eat. Then there was the cake, brought blazing from the house, and Lotte cut it herself while Ida and Farmor and Fru Fugl and Tove brought trays of ice cream. And then came the gifts.

Almost everything was for traveling. Handkerchiefs and a comb and a soapdish and several bright scarves and even a small leather kit with a toothbrush that folded up and toothpaste and everything. Fru Fugl gave her a little red book with a lock on it—a diary—and Lisa a book for autographs, which already had a page filled out by every member of the class.

Then came the big box from America. It was fun to open with everybody watching. And of all odd things, it was not just a gift for Lotte but a gift for her to give to the others. It was in two parts, one a huge puzzle map of the United States, with each state its own color and bearing a picture of its flower and its flag. Putting it together was a game that would be "good for geography" as Patrick had written

on his card. The other gift was a globe of the world. It had a light that turned on inside to show all the different countries and stood on a pedestal that turned around and around.

"How wonderful for our class!" Fru Fugl said. And she asked if she might read a letter Mor had written about it. "We thought Lotte would like to leave something for the class. And both Pat and I remembered something about maps—how, as he says, they are apt to be like menus in a language you can't understand and do little for your appetite. But when you study them and then eventually go to the places they symbolize—and we feel that every one of these children will someday come to America or go to other wonderful places around the world—the maps become real, little lines become mountains, the blue spaces sea, and the spots that are cities become streets and buildings and adventures and people who become friends. Our birthday wish for Lotte, please tell her for us when these gifts are opened, is that America may become another home and not only a map and that she must invite all of you to come and see for yourselves."

Everybody sat still, listening. And then Fru Fugl laughed and said, "Well! Thank you, Lotte, and thanks to your parents." And everybody stood up, and in two minutes they were choosing sides for a game, and it was late afternoon before the last guest went down the road, and Lotte and Lisa took their tea in the little house.

CHAPTER TWELVE

※

News and a Witch

"Fru Fugl says we're going over the Lillebelt Bridge because we're going to stop in Odense and see where H. C. Andersen lived, and then we'll go on the Big Belt ferry from Nyborg—"

"I thought we would go on the ferry from Grenaa—"

"*Nej,* that's on the way home. She told me so."

"*Nej—ja!* We'll see!" Poor Fru Fugl had no peace about the excursion until she received all the plans from Hr. Axel and called a special meeting of all those who were able to go. Twenty-five children had the consent of their parents and the funds to go along with it and sleeping bags and all. Fru Fugl pointed their way on the huge map of Denmark. "You see, we will go across Fünen on the way to Copenhagen and stop at Odense and then go south to see the old Manor House Egeskov and then up to the ferry. See—we will have dinner on the boat—and then we will drive on and spend the first night at the hostel in Roskilde."

"Don't we see the castle at Nyborg?"

"Will we see the Viking Ship?"

"We can't do *everything* on one trip! Leave something for the next time—"

Lotte thought, *there is no next time for me.* She listened

to the talk around her without saying a word. Everybody was so full of excitement about the excursion that the end of school seemed to mean nothing at all. There had been a fine assembly on the last day; she had presented the globe and the map to the school and everybody clapped, and then the band played, and they all got their report cards as they marched out of the door into the sun. For everybody else it was just another ending of another school year, and they looked with joy to the wonders of summer. But Lotte felt that some terrible witch had spun a web about her heart, and it beat in a muffled tangle that was not pain and yet was a kind of pain. Even Lisa did not seem to think about anything but the trip; ever since she got that prize, she seemed to think she was the queen-pin of everybody! Her whole trip was paid for, even the whole day at Tivoli—and she would have the first-prize essay in the newspaper the very day they all arrived in Copenhagen. Of course, the poems would be printed too. But Lotte did not like to think that Lisa's essay would say, "First Prize," and her poem only, "Third Prize."

"Fru Fugl told my Mor that maybe Hr. Axel is going to meet us at Odense," Lisa said importantly one day. "And we'll meet the Mayor of Odense and Hr. Larsen, who's the director of the H. C. Andersen *Hus* and the Museum of Odense and everything—"

"And he might bring a photographer. We'll all have our pictures in the newspaper," Ole said.

"The way *I* did," Lotte said. But nobody was paying much attention to anything over and done with—or to anything to come after the excursion to Copenhagen.

Ole said, "Hr. Axel told my Farmor that we might be

given a key to the city when we get to the old West Gate.
That's where H. C. Andersen came in when he went to seek
his fortune." Ole, Lotte knew, had a new dream now. He
too would be a writer—hadn't his poem won a prize?—and
go to the big city and make his fortune. Maybe he would
get to be famous. Looking at his excited face, she knew
what he was thinking.

But nobody seemed to care what she was thinking. Even
Lisa, even when she came over and found Lotte and Farmor
in the middle of packing. Farmor kept saying, "Why don't
you leave Lisa that? It's too much to take, really—you won't
use it much again—" Games and old dolls and scrapbooks
and books. "Your mother said your room over there isn't
very big—and not much closet space in those new apartments."

Lisa was there the day Farmor brought the locket down
from the Lotte Room.

"You might as well take this with you," Farmor said, as
casually as she might say take a book or a pair of skates or
anything.

"Farmor—" Lotte said, and she felt pale all over. "I was
supposed to get the locket when I'm *confirmed!*"

So matter-of-fact Farmor was. "I know, but if you're not
going to be confirmed here, that's that," she said. "I'd rather
you took it than trust it to the mails." And she laid it among
Lotte's things in the top of the trunk.

Lotte could not say a word. And when Farmor went out
of the room, she stood looking at the lovely old plush box
in which the locket was kept. It looked all wrong away
from the big chest. And how wrong, how very wrong it

would look in a room higher than larks with no old chest
to lie in! She walked slowly to the trunk and picked up the
box and opened it slowly, feeling as sober and sorrowful as
if she were about to say a prayer for somebody who had
just died. Not one of those Lottes would like it, she thought,
for the locket to leave Denmark. *Never mind,* she thought,
and looked swiftly around, for it seemed that she spoke to
all six of the ghosts and Farmor too. *I'll never never never
take the locket out of Denmark.*

It was the most solemn promise she had ever made in
her life.

The very next day Mor's special delivery letter came. Lotte
ripped it open and began to read aloud as she and Farmor
always did. "Lotte darling, I am hurrying to tell you some
wonderful news. Just before next Christmas—" Lotte's eyes
had raced ahead, and she stopped reading.

Farmor looked up. And Lotte felt her heart begin to beat
harder all of a sudden as if she had been riding her bicycle
the length of the lane. Her breathing stopped, deep in her
throat, and she swallowed.

"What is it?" Farmor asked, alarmed.

Lotte tried to begin again. "Just before Christmas—" and
paused once more because of the painful breathing. Then
her voice came small. "—we will have a new member of
our family! Isn't that wonderful? Patrick and I are both so
very happy and know you will be happy too. We wanted you
to have the news to tell Lisa—maybe you'll have a little
brother too. Imagine, a real family at last."

Ida had stopped to listen. Her face was one huge smile.
And Farmor said, "How wonderful!"

Lotte smiled too, but it was as if her face were made of

stone. And after that, as the news got around the neighbor-hood—Mor had told several of her old friends, Tove and Fru Fugl among them—she had to smile and smile and *smile*. She heard Farmor say to Tove, "Now I'll *have* to go over there, won't I ? Especially if I have a grandson after all this time."

It didn't even seem to occur to her that this baby wouldn't be her grandson at all. It was not Far's baby, only Mor's. But when Lotte reminded Farmor of this one day, Farmor laughed and said, "I just feel that any child of your mother's is a grandchild of mine. Gerda has been my daughter for a long time." She frowned then. "Lotte, sometimes I think you're actually a bit jealous of that baby already," she said.

Just before Christmas, Mor had said. She wouldn't be feeling much like getting presents and decorations and a tree, Lotte thought. And anyway, people in America didn't celebrate Christmas the way they did in Denmark. Nobody put out porridge for the *Nisse*, Patrick had said. And there was a fire law in New York City that nobody must have living light on a Christmas tree. The thought of a tree with-out candles burning on it gave Lotte the most un-Christmasy feeling she ever had in her life.

But then, she thought, marking out June 20 on her cal-endar, and June 21, and June 22, and then June 23—maybe that was because of the June feeling everywhere, the lane ablaze with roses, the woods and meadows bright with green and now beginning to shine with poppies. The sun at four in the afternoon was as high and fine as noonday, and once more the nights shimmered with the magic light of mid-summer.

In the back yard at Lisa's house, Palle and Svend and

Knud and Harald worked most of the afternoon, making their witch to burn on Midsummer's Eve. Palle made the face, as ugly as possible, out of wire and bits of paper and paste. Knud made her hat tall and pointed, and Lisa and Lotte fixed her clothes from some old rags in the attic. They put them on a big crossed stick, the way you do a scarecrow, and on top of the ugly head were hung long gray skeins of tangled wool for hair. She was the ugliest, realest-looking witch any of them had ever seen.

"It's too bad to burn her, she's so wonderfully ugly," Lotte said.

While they worked, Lisa's Mor brought out cookies and bottles of cold pop. It was always hard to choose between the gold and the red, so Lisa and Lotte took different ones and then switched, halfway. They had done that ever since they could remember.

They cycled all together to find a place for their fire, on a hill. The younger boys carried paper and wood in their big baskets. Palle carried the witch on her broom. Everywhere they looked, people were laying fires.

"If only it doesn't rain!" It was like a chant, from group to group. Almost every year it rained. Anxiously they looked at the high clouds that were sweeping grandly from sea to sea.

They made a pile of paper and wood higher than Palle, with the witch on top against the sky. They waited, laughing and talking and playing games, until the sun lowered. And at last Lisa's parents came, bringing Farmor, and, of course, huge baskets of food. Finally there was a spark at a distance. And another. And another.

"Shall we light ours now?" Palle cried.

They stood in a circle, as close as possible, while he leaned over the pile with a lighted taper. The flame caught in the paper and blazed up, caught another piece, rose among the sticks. Looking balefully down, the witch seemed to grin and frown together from her perch above the flame. Lotte gazed up at her and shivered. "Did they really burn *real* witches in the old time?" she whispered to Farmor.

She knew the answer, of course. She had asked the same question every year, and every year had the same answer. "They say so. People believed strange things for more years than anybody knows. Some say it was a charm to make the crops grow well during the summer. And some say we have it all mixed up with Walpurgis, the First of May, when witches were supposed to ride to a secret meeting on Brocken, a high mountain peak goodness knew where. People said, looking up at the burning witch, 'She will carry our troubles away to Brocken.' And somebody always asked, 'Where is Brocken?' and somebody would answer, 'It's only the place one sends witches. Maybe it is nowhere so our troubles are gone forever.'

"Now," Farmor said, giving Lotte a little squeeze, "I think the witches are burned to remind us that troubles never last forever, and we must burn them away."

Lisa's Far stared up at the witch as the flames crept upward. Her sleeves began to flap in the heat, as if she waved her arms. "My father used to say that people believed in fairies and witches in the old time because of the shadows of candles dancing on the walls every night. Have you noticed how candles make shadows and witches in the corners?"

In firelight there were dancing shadows too. They seemed

alive and yet were not alive. The flames caught at the witch's hair. She was a blazing pillar now. Her face! A column of flame burst out of the very peak of her hat. LillePer stood gazing up, his eyes wide and unmoving. There she stood for a flaming moment, and then suddenly she began to crumble, to fall. The pole had burnt through. As the remains of the witch disappeared into the heap of coals, Lisa's Far said, "During the war she had black mustaches! It made the German soldiers very angry."

The fire sank down, and pillows and blankets were spread around it on the ground and a cloth for the food. As they ate and drank, gazing at the bed of warm coals, they could hear voices from other fires, and presently somebody began to sing. From fire to fire, voices joined together. "To St. Hans." "In Denmark Was I Born." And for the children, "Stork, Stork, Longlegs, Where Have You Been for So Long?"

Palle built the fire up again when they had finished eating, and they lay around together on the ground. Farmor told stories about the old time, about the Vikings and about the days when people worshipped Odin and Thor. And in her own childhood there had been a nightwatchman in the town, walking along in wooden shoes that clopped on the cobblestones. "He sang a different song for every hour," she said. "When I visited my grandmother in Ribe, I used to lie awake to hear him. But I never could stay awake past ten o'clock. 'Heard ye the clock strike ten? This hour is worth the knowing . . . the time is here and going . . .' And then I would fall asleep."

Lotte felt that she too would fall asleep from the comfort

of her head in Farmor's lap and from gazing into the fire. Stars were wavering through the pale and smoky light. LillePer sat on his mother's lap, gazing with wide sleepy eyes at the fire and at the sky. Lovers strolled by, hand in hand. It was true, here together all the troubles in the world seemed to fly away.

No matter what, I belong here, Lotte thought. Lisa's little brother is all the brother I need. Anyway, by the time Mor's new baby got to be Per's age, she would be eighteen! Imagine being eighteen! She would be a student then, in the university. But in America there were no student caps, Patrick had said. How terrible never to wear a student cap and go riding around *Kongens Nytorv*, the King's New Square, in a flowered cart! Looking up into Farmor's kindly face and around her at the faces in the firelight, she thought, Now I don't need to go! Mor will have other children— she won't need me. I can stay here and be Farmor's child. The thought filled her with happiness—and yet with sadness as well, so that she felt her sadness and gladness stirred together in an impossible stew. She felt like crying, and yet a vast relief flooded over her. She would write a letter to Mor just before the time came for the ship to sail—and it wouldn't do to tell Farmor until the very last moment either. She would say, "Mor has an American child; she doesn't need a Danish child as well." She would explain that she could never take Lotte's locket out of Denmark where it belonged. And how could she leave it behind? Now, she thought, staring at the fire and inventing the letter she would write to Mor, I will stay here with Farmor, who has nobody but me. I can stay here and finish school and go to the university and then live all my life at Lottegaard. Perhaps I will be married and then— She thought suddenly of Ole. She could marry him; there had never been any other boy in her mind when she thought about marrying, and how happy he would be to have Lottegaard so close to his inn! They would write poems—they could have some of their poems painted on the walls like those telling the story of Tove and her man in one of the rooms at the inn. Her whole life unfolded before her, peaceful and bright in the firelight. She closed her eyes. Songs floated in the shimmering air. She would say to Farmor the last day, "I am not going. I have told Mor—it is all right."

Her trunk would go to the boat, of course, but let it go to America without her. She smiled at the thought of Mor receiving the trunk and having to send it back again.

"Patrick," Mor would say, weeping, "here is Lotte's trunk. Here are her dolls and her dresses and everything—but no Lotte—" As if she had died and gone to heaven.

Suddenly a drop of water plopped onto her face. Her eyes flew open. A flock of clouds was rushing over, and people were scrambling, laughing, gathering things together. LillePer began to cry. The rain fell faster, and they all began to run, dragging the blankets, piling things into their baskets. The little lights of dozens of bicycles shone along the road.

"Well, it could have been worse! Last year on Midsummer's Eve it drowned the fire, and the witches were only half burned—"

Fires in every direction were sinking, growing duller and duller. They were like mysterious eyes looking out of the earth.

CHAPTER THIRTEEN

The Great Excursion

The big bus stood in the schoolyard across from the inn. It looked like a summer camp. Everybody had a suitcase and a sleeping bag, and some brought guitars and radios and cameras and bags of sandwiches and baskets of fruit and all sorts of special things for fun on the road. Parents and brothers and sisters and friends swarmed to say good-by. When Fru Fugl called, "All aboard!" it was a marvelous scramble, with kissing and laughing and singing and shouting good-by. You would have thought the excursion was going around the world.

Lisa's Mor held Lotte in her big warm embrace. "Lotte dear—we'll miss you so much! But have a happy time, and take your Mor our love—and Patrick—"

Lotte smiled to herself. Nobody knew she would be coming back, even Farmor, who sat with Finn in the car with the trunk in the back. They would go to Copenhagen in the car right along with the bus. And Tove, too, to help Fru Fugl take charge of the children.

Lisa said, "Lotte, you can have the window. You're saying good-by to everything—" which was very sweet of her. After all, she did not know, either, and it was not yet time to tell her. Again and again, Lotte had been tempted to say, "Lisa,

I'm not going—" but she was not sure Lisa could keep such a secret. And the important thing was not to let Farmor know until the very last. Maybe, Lotte thought, her face against the window, pretending to say a sad good-by to everything along the road the way Mor had done, she had better pretend to be lost again for an hour or so, just when it was time to go to the boat. She would be with Farmor in the hotel the last night, and she could go downstairs on the elevator and walk up St. Annae Plads, and maybe she could go into a shop—and later, when everybody was all upset and the ship had gone and the police were looking for her as they did before, she would go back to the hotel and say, "Here I am!" And maybe they would put her picture in the paper again, beside her poem, and say in the headlines, *"Lille pige* refuses to go to America! Must stay at home in Denmark and wear Lotte's locket!"

It was an exciting thought. Everybody would forget all about the excursion and the essay and poems, and Hr. Axel would write a story just for her. Sad for Lisa and Ole, in a way, but then—what could you do?

"There's Randers," Lisa said, against her ear. "Already!" And then they began to laugh, and everybody was plastered against the window because Finn had caught up with the bus and was trying to pass. The little old car kept right abreast of the huge, roaring bus. Finn's face was red with laughter, and Farmor and Tove waved and waved.

How lovely the countryside was today! They passed Randers and made for Skanderborg and Horsens and Vejle and came to Middelfart over the Little Belt Bridge, which took them to the fairy island of Fünen, where Hans Christian Andersen had been born. Lotte had to admit that Fünen was even lovelier countryside than she knew in Jutland, and the road was lined with fine old farms and brightly colored timbered cottages. She and Lisa made up a game like the one Patrick had played with her before, scoring windmills and cows and horses and pigs and dogs and the highest score of all for storks. They saw four before the number of houses increased, and they saw smokestacks ahead and factories and towers that meant Odense, next to Copenhagen and Aarhus, the biggest town in Denmark.

"We will spend an hour here—*we have only an hour*—stay together." Fru Fugl warned everybody that if they were not at the bus at eleven sharp, they would be left. "We must make the ferry at Nyborg by noon," she said, "so at each stop stay in line please."

It wasn't much fun to see sights in a long line. In the wonderful little house on Jensenstraede where H. C. Andersen had lived were rooms of things—books and letters and drawings and cuttings and hundreds of things he had himself owned and saved. Lotte wanted to stop and read every card and look carefully at every article, but the long line moved along in front of Fru Fugl. "Someday we'll come back and stay and stay," she whispered to Lisa.

"When you come for a visit," Lisa said.

Then they went to St. Knud's Church where the fairy-story writer had once walked down the aisle on his confirmation day making his new boots squeak so people would notice him. A fine statue stood in the Hans Christian Andersen Garden behind the church, and across the street was the little house where he had lived with his mother and his shoemaker-father. There was a little gooseberry bush in the yard, and Lotte wondered whether it was the very one he had seen and written about.

"Time to go!" Fru Fugl was really an old hen today. But they were all glad to see the bus and eager for the sight of the pretty ferry waiting for them, its flags flying. There was a long line of cars and trucks coming off and another long line waiting to go aboard. When the bus moved on, it was tucked in neatly with several other buses but so tightly that it was difficult to open the door wide enough to get out.

"Attention!" Fru Fugl called, and the driver gave them instructions. They might go up on deck and walk about and eat and do exactly as they liked, but the moment the signal for landing came, they were to return and be ready in their seats for disembarking. "Anybody not aboard when it is time to drive off the boat will be left. We can't hold up traffic," the driver said. So they swarmed up the steep narrow stairs and came out into the fresh air and the bright sea-sun.

"Oh, dear," Lotte heard a woman say to her husband, "There's another of those *awful* excursions!"

Lisa and Lotte stuck their tongues out at her behind her back. They were not an awful excursion at all, but a very orderly one with Fru Fugl in charge. And when they marched into the dining room, they tried to make Fru Fugl proud of them, standing quietly in line for their *smørrebrød*. There was one little trouble when some of the children fought over who would have window seats, but Fru Fugl settled it quickly. "If you had a window seat in the bus, take an inside seat here," she said.

There were dozens of sandwiches to choose from, great

bright trays of ham and cheese and beef and pork and tongue and lobster and shrimp and *rødspaette* and every kind of herring you could imagine.

"Let's each take two different things and then divide," Lisa whispered. "That way we'll have four different kinds."

So they did. And they divided the pop, as always. Then they had two kinds of sweet cakes to finish and carried them along outside to the railing where they watched Funen shrinking behind them and Zealand growing larger ahead. Gulls wheeled over them, squalling for cake and plunging into the water for the bits they threw. And before they could believe it, they were summoned into the bus once more and were riding out into the sun at Korsør. Then came the great wide highway toward Copenhagen, which was now only sixty-seven kilometers away. They were almost too impatient to stop at the great cathedral at Roskilde where most of the Danish kings were buried, from the Viking Harald I to Christian X. The most interesting thing to Lotte was not the tombs but the wonderful clock with St. George coming out to fight the dragon whenever an hour struck.

Lisa was so excited that she was the first back on the bus. "I can't believe it—Copenhagen!" she said. No longer did she offer to let Lotte sit by the window. Copenhagen was her prize from the moment she caught sight of the first factories, all along the road, and then the green of Frederiksberg Gardens and the entrance to the zoo. "It's too late for the zoo tonight," Fru Fugl said, and one could hear the cross weariness in her voice. "It's time for bed all around— but the first thing in the morning—"

The bus was moving in the traffic, and all eyes were

glued to the windows, to the endless buildings and the street lamps as bright as day and the trolley cars sometimes so close they could almost be touched. The bus arrived at the hostel near the University, turning in through a narrow gate that seemed to threaten to scrape off its windows. They stood in a bricked court—and there, smiling in the sudden shine of electric lights, stood Hr. Axel. Beside him was the cameraman Lotte remembered.

"File off quietly. We'll assign you to your places, and we'll bring your sleeping bags." Poor Fru Fugl was still hopping. But she looked happy when they all stood in the bright courtyard where they would sleep, and Hr. Axel made a little speech. While he spoke, a flashbulb went off and they squealed and laughed. "Is that for the newspaper?"

"We haven't planned anything after supper tonight," Hr. Axel said. "Tomorrow is another day!" He had an envelope for each child, and while they ate at a long table, they all looked at wonderful illustrated folders.

An excursion was a kind of glorified school. Hr. Axel and Fru Fugl told everybody exactly what they would do tomorrow and the day after tomorrow. Rosenborg, Amalienborg (and Hr. Axel smiled at Lotte as he said they would be at the King's palace at noon to see the guard changed), Christiansborg, where the *Rigsdag,* the Danish parliament, would be meeting tomorrow and where they would go down into the ruins of Bishop Absalon's first castle, built in 1167, and up into the Royal State Apartments where the King and Queen gave their dinner parties. And then, at last, Tivoli.

"You must all stay together. We can't be looking for stray children all over Copenhagen! We have provided these caps for you, with red ribbons, and we'll divide you into special twos—"

Everybody laughed when Lisa said, "I'll keep a good eye on Lotte!"

While they ate, Finn and Farmor and Tove arrived, and then what a bustle getting the sleeping bags arranged in rows, one for the girls and one for the boys, and out came the toothbrushes, and it was a camp again. It all seemed to be going by like a swift dream, half unreal. When they were ready for bed, they sang together in the courtyard, looking up at the Round Tower. Then they tucked themselves into their bags.

"Oh, Lotte, isn't it wonderful! And tomorrow night, supper at Tivoli. *Tivoli!*" Lisa reached out and took Lotte's hand in the half-light.

"No whispering!"

The sounds of the city were different and exciting as the big yard fell into silence. A clock bonged out ten o'clock. The City Hall? And there was another one—some church near by?

"Lisa?" Lotte moved closer to whisper. But there was no answer. How could Lisa fall asleep so easily when she was so excited? Lotte felt the familiar crawl of nerves along her legs and arms. Day after tomorrow, the ship. Maybe Tivoli was the place to be lost—she could slip off into the crowd. But no, maybe early in the morning when she was supposed to go to the ship. She thought of how it had been before and to be lost at night would be worse. It might be fun to be lost with somebody else—maybe Lisa! I'll tell Lisa when we're in Tivoli, she thought. I'll tell her I've decided not to go, after all, and exactly what I want to do. She'll think it's fun to get into the newspaper the way I did before. Her mind skipped the time of being lost straight to the time of being found. She was standing with Lisa in front of a huge crowd.

If only Lisa had not gone to sleep so soon.

But now she herself slipped into a dream, and then she heard her own name, and Lisa was poking her awake. The place was coming alive, exploding with laughter and talk and water running and Fru Fugl talking and the good, welcome smell of bacon frying.

It was five o'clock before they got to Tivoli. What a day! They climbed the Round Tower and Our Saviour's Tower and saw the World Clock and both palaces and the Crown Jewels. They ate at a wonderful place that had menus a yard long and sold five hundred different kinds of sandwiches.

But at last they were going through the turnstile into the fairyland of Tivoli. Patrick had said there was nothing in the whole world like Tivoli. He said there was Coney Island in New York, and it had a few of the same things—but nothing and nowhere could be compared with this piece of wonder smack in the middle of Copenhagen. It was built on some of the old city ramparts, now become gardens and lawns, with an old moat, which had become a charming lake alive with birds. It had a concert hall and dance halls and an open-air ballet and—imagine—twenty-three places to eat. Some were simple little places where people brought their own baskets of food and bought only a little pop or

beer to go with it. And there were fine places as elegant and
expensive as the best restaurants in Copenhagen. There was
a flea-circus and a fun-house and a place where you could
smash plates with baseballs if you felt like it. There was a
little railroad train going around and around to show people
everything, and a golden carriage you could ride in and
pretend to be a queen. The Boys' Royal Guard and band
were dressed exactly like the King's own.

The first thing Lisa wanted to do was ride on the Ferris
wheel. It was a wonderful big wheel with swinging baskets
to sit in and huge colored balloons over every one. Around
and around they went, and there were so many of their
classmates on the wheel at the same time that they waved
at each other and swung the baskets up and down.

"Isn't it wonderful?" Lisa's cheeks were scarlet with pleasure. "It's even more wonderful than I expected. It seems
like a dream, doesn't it—Tivoli and everything?"

"*Ja.* But it isn't. Do you remember that H. C. Andersen
story, *It's Perfectly True? He* thought fairy things were true,
he always did, Farmor says she's sure of it—and he said his
life, his *true life,* was really a fairy tale."

The switchback came next. What wild yelling when the
cars went hurtling down the steep places! Then everybody
went on little boats that wound through caverns underground. As they slid along through the lovely colored lights
that were reflected in the water, Lotte thought of telling
Lisa about her plan. But she got only as far as saying, "Lisa
—tomorrow when the boat goes—"

"Don't let's talk about it, Lotte," Lisa said. "I told Mor I

wasn't even going to think about your going but was going *to enjoy every single minute* we had left." Her eyes looked shiny, as if tears stood just behind them. "Let's just make it as perfect as we can, shall we? And sometime, the way Mor says, you'll come back for a visit. And maybe sometime I can come to America. If I save—and *save*—"

Their little boat swung into the last stretch and moved through a little gate, and they were helped out by the attendant.

"Now I'm hungry," Lisa said. "You wouldn't believe I'd eaten all those sandwiches such a little while ago."

It had been arranged that everybody should report to Fru Fugl at the statue of Pierrot. It was a very old tradition for people to meet there beside the statue of the great actor, who had been beloved of Danish children for fifty years. So now they reported and saw some of their friends, and then they were off again. A wonderful pastry and chocolate shop had been pointed out to them by Hr. Axel, and why shouldn't Lisa use her key to Tivoli? Part of her prize was a long ticket that bought for her anything she wanted in any shop or restaurant and took her on any ride or to any concert. So they sat by a small round table, and each ate two huge dishes of ice cream. Each dish had three scoops of ice cream, one with chocolate on it, one strawberry, and one lemon with a sprinkling of nuts on top and half a banana arranged on either side. Then they had cakes, lovely little frosted cakes in different colors that they could carry off in a bag and eat as they watched the flea circus.

"*Loppe—loppe—loppe!*" That was the man announcing the flea circus. And there were the most wonderful little fleas in the world! Some rode tiny bicycles, some rode in tiny golden carriages, and one could walk a tightrope upside down.

When they came out, it was time for the big vaudeville program to begin. A great crowd of people stood watching, and every seat in the center of the place was filled. It would have been hard to see, but the stage was high. There were jugglers, who could keep about forty balls in the air at the same time. There were people who did tricks on a high wire and then swung out over the audience, doing tricks the whole time.

"Here, I've bought some popcorn," Lisa said. Lotte hadn't even noticed that she had slipped away. So they watched and ate. Then it was time for the famous pantomime in the little theatre with a huge mechanical peacock for a curtain. Once more they stood watching, but this time a guard came and made the tall people in front move back so the children could all see.

As they waited for the peacock's tail to open and reveal the scene behind, they looked for their friends in the crowd. And almost at once, they saw Hr. Axel and Farmor and Tove, who had bought seats. "I couldn't stand up another minute," Farmor said, when Lotte and Lisa came close to greet them. "I feel ashamed to sit with so many standing, but if I stand another minute, I'll faint dead away."

"I, too," Tove said.

Hr. Axel smiled at Lotte. "This is a good finale for your Danish life, isn't it? We were just now talking about it," he said. "Do you remember coming here before and sitting with your mother right here where we are now?"

She did not remember. And no wonder! He said she had been a year old, and her father had been there too. "I think perhaps you remember in your blood, the way most Danes do," he said. "Tivoli is something we all know—every one of us—from the day we arrive with the stork."

They all laughed. None of them were so little now that they thought storks fetched babies from the sky. The orchestra was tuning up, and *ja,* it did sound familiar, all of it, and when they began to fiddle away and the bright tail of the peacock parted to show Pierrot putting to sea in a barrel, it was as if she had seen it all before. Then Harlequin came in with his magic stick, shining all over, and there was dear Columbine in her short skirts, shimmering into a dance. How beautiful it was! Lisa reached out and took Lotte's hand, and of course, before very long she was saying once more, "Isn't it wonderful?"

They emptied the bag of cakes between them and then wandered off once more toward another burst of music, which turned out to be a concert in a band-shell. They went next to the lake and rowed around among ducks and swans and water lilies, trailing their fingers in a drip of lights that moved beside the boats.

They ate a bag of peanuts and caramels and then walked clear around the lake to look at the nests the ducks had built here and there.

Then they went into a small red house that looked as if it might belong to the Gingerbread Witch and had sandwiches and hot chocolate.

"I'm not very hungry any more," Lotte said, giggling.

"Neither am I," said Lisa. "But I'm thirsty!" So they had pop, and when they had emptied their bottles, they went back to report once more at the statue of Pierrot.

There were Fru Fugl and Hr. Axel and Farmor and Tove, all ready for the day to be brought to an end. "I was never so tired in all my life," Tove said.

Farmor leaned to Lotte and said, "Don't you think you'd better come with me to the hotel tonight? You won't get much rest with that crowd in that awful sleeping bag of yours."

But Lisa heard. "Oh, no!" she cried, in dismay. "This is

our *last night!*" And she made it sound, indeed, as if it were the last night in this world.

"Well—it is my last night with Lotte too, Lisa," Farmor said.

Lotte stood looking at one and the other and at Hr. Axel who seemed interested to see what she would decide to do. If he knew what she was planning, she thought. It was because of the plan that she said, "Farmor, if you don't really mind—I sleep fine in the sleeping bag—"

"We were going to climb up the tower and see the fireworks," Fru Fugl said. "But of course, if you think—" She looked at Farmor, understanding.

"If you don't really mind, Farmor—" Lotte said again. "Anyway, you'll go right to sleep if you're so tired."

That was certainly true. Farmor laughed and said, "Very well, then," and kissed Lotte good night. Lotte moved into the long line, and they filed gaily through the gate and found the bus waiting once again.

Everybody was quiet for a change, all tired. Lotte thought, Now is the time to tell Lisa—but Lisa had some secrets too that were hard to keep. "Lotte, did you know we've made posters for you? One says, '*Farvel,* Lotte! Come back soon!' And we're all going to sing and wave our flags as your ship sails, just the way we did on Liberation Day!"

The bus moved through the streets, turning corners and bumping over cobblestones. Every time it bumped, something bumped in the very center of Lotte, and it all began to gather together and then seemed to swell in her throat.

"Oh, *dear*—Lisa, I think I'm going to be sick," she said.

It was right in the middle of the palace yard at Christians-borg. The bus suddenly stopped for another bus and then started again. A pain struck Lotte square under her heart. *"Lisa—"* she said.

Lisa held her head, and Fru Fugl rushed to help, and everybody watched—how awful! But Lotte was too sick to care.

CHAPTER FOURTEEN

The Most Incredible Thing

Dimly, as they waited for the doctor, Lotte heard Lisa answering the questions. "Well—pop and popcorn and sandwiches and cake—and—*ja,* candy. Ice cream—"

Before the doctor came, Farmor appeared in a terrible state, and then everything was in an awful muddle. Lotte heard her telling the doctor, "She's sailing to America in the morning!"

And he said the most amazing thing, as if he had known all along what her plan was. "I really doubt whether this little lady is going to feel like traveling for a while." He gave her some medicine while everybody stood around, whispering and watching, and then Hr. Axel picked Lotte up, wrapped in a blanket, and they carried her off. Three times on the way to the hotel she was sick again. But now there were no more peanuts or popcorn, only an evil water that seemed to bubble up from a place deeper than any place she ever knew she had. How wonderful it was to be put into the soft bed with her head on two pillows! And then there was only a lamp burning dimly, far off beyond a door. Farmor was saying something, and the doctor was saying something, and a telephone rang, but she no longer cared. She only wanted to sleep and sleep—

Lotte opened her eyes. In her dream Mor had been talking to Hr. Axel and Farmor, and now Lotte saw that she was not awake, after all, but still dreaming. Because there was Mor, smiling. Yet the room and the window and everything seemed real.

"Lotte—" Mor leaned down, gathering her close.

It was the realest dream she had ever had. She *felt* Mor,

and the sweet scent she always used was vivid, near, as real as real.

"I think she thinks she's still dreaming. And no wonder." That was Hr. Axel, standing not far away. He laughed.

"Do you think I'm a dream, darling?" Mor held her off, looking anxious. She was the same, but different. She wore a dress Lotte had never seen, full and flowered, with some of the flowers exactly the color of her eyes. "You won't believe how I got here so fast," she said.

Farmor was there too, just beyond. She stood by Hr. Axel, and they were both smiling. Everybody was smiling, even the maid who kept dabbing at her eyes with her apron, just as Ida always did.

"I *flew!*" Mor said. "Imagine. I was so much more scared about your being sick than scared I might fall out of the sky—"

"I'll never get used to such things, I'm too old for it," Farmor said. "It took you less time, Gerda, to come from New York than it took us to come to Copenhagen!"

"A ship takes as many *days* as one of those jets takes *hours*," Hr. Axel said. "I am beginning to believe in men on the moon. I used to think it could never be, but now I wonder."

"But six *months* in the old days. It used to take six solid months on a sailing ship," Farmor said.

Now Lotte knew absolutely for sure that Mor's hand and the pressure of her arm were real. She looked round-faced and plump and happy. *Ja*—so happy!

"Where's Patrick?" she asked.

She saw Mor glance quickly at Farmor. "He's in New

York," she said. "He couldn't get away in five minutes the way I could, but he's coming soon, if he can. And if he can't, you and I can manage by ourselves, can't we? He put me on that plane for Copenhagen one hour after we heard you couldn't come on the ship. And he said, 'You go over there quick and bring back our little girl!'"

Lotte lay still. She could feel a strange throbbing deep inside where her heart was. Imagine Patrick doing such a wonderful thing.

"I don't think I'll really be afraid to fly again," Mor said. "It was just like a big ship, only as smooth as lying in bed. Those marvelous jets! Sometimes I could hardly hear the engine or anything, and they played the gentlest music, and I didn't even need my pill to get to sleep. So restful!"

"When I met you, I thought you looked like somebody getting up from a good night's sleep," Hr. Axel said.

"And I was. Except for worrying about Lotte, and I knew"—she was smiling—"I really knew why she was sick. Every letter she wrote—" They were talking over Lotte's head, as if she were not there, but she didn't mind. "Every letter, I knew how hard it was for her to come away. She was worried over the locket, and over Farmor, and Lisa, and everything. School. Even the climate and the *birds,* for goodness sakes! And whether Americans had Christmas! Patrick couldn't get over *that.*"

They were all laughing, and at her, but it didn't matter because it was gentle laughter, and now she could say it all to everybody, and the pain was disappearing entirely, and she sat up, smiling too and listening.

"Guess what was the first thing I saw when I woke up?" Mor asked. "It seemed to me I'd barely slept, and suddenly

I woke up and saw that it was bright day already. Down below was Denmark. I called the hostess and said, 'Surely that's not Denmark already?' And she said, '*Ja,* and in a moment you will see Copenhagen.' And there it was. I could see the towers, every single one, and then I saw this hotel, just a glimpse, and I knew I'd be seeing you in a little while."

She leaned down to give Lotte a kiss. "And Hr. Axel didn't let me lose any time—he was right there and whisked me in to town and up on the elevator. It was like something out of H. C. Andersen! Do you remember that wonderful piece of his, 'Thousands of Years From Now'? He knew people would be flying and that the world was a magic place, didn't he? But he didn't have any idea that it would be less than a *hundred* years—"

"I often think how much he'd have loved flying," Farmor said. "After all, he had one of his heroes flying around the world in a trunk."

Suddenly the telephone rang.

"I'll bet that's Patrick," Mor said. "He was going to call the first thing this morning." She reached for the telephone beside the bed, but Lotte touched her arm.

"Mor, may I answer?" she asked.

Without a word, Mor handed her the receiver, and they all listened. And yes, it was Patrick. His voice boomed out as clearly as if he were in the next room and not over thousands of miles of wild sea away.

"This is Lotte— *Ja,* I'm a lot better. Mor is here, she came this morning and— *Ja,* she says it was wonderful, and she wasn't afraid at all."

They could all hear the booming of his voice. And then,

"That would be wonderful! Oh, *ja, ja,* that's *wonderful—*"

Then he was speaking again, and Lotte's face had an unbelieving wonder in it, and her voice too when she asked, "Would you like to talk to Mor?"

Farmor and Hr. Axel began to laugh. What a question! And Mor was talking to him, then, telling him all about everything. But Lotte could not keep the wonderful news, and whispered, "Farmor—Hr. Axel—Pat's coming in a few days, and we're all going out to Rebild Park before we go home to America and celebrate the Fourth of July!"

Mor was smiling when she hung up. "Think of that!" She too looked unbelieving.

"Well, Lotte, you'll have a big mouthful of America before ever you cross the sea," Hr. Axel said. "I'm going out to report that celebration. Last year there were 15,000 Americans at Rebild, and it was wonderful to see the two flags flying together and to hear both Danes and Americans singing their two anthems, first one and then the other."

"After all, most of them belong to both countries, don't they?" Farmor asked. "They're mostly Danes whose ancestors went to America as emigrants a long time ago."

"Or not so long ago," Hr. Axel said.

Lotte knew what he was thinking. "And they took their 'invisible baggage'—all of them, didn't they? All the things they got from their grandmothers and their great-great-great-*great—*"

"Invisible baggage?" Mor asked. "What an odd thing to say, Lotte!" Mor laughed the way she always did when Lotte had said something clever. "It sounds like something from H. C. Andersen!"

"So it does." Hr. Axel and Lotte smiled at each other. "So many things nowadays seem like something from fairy-land, don't they? Yet—as one of his stories says, 'It's all perfectly true.' Even the most incredible things."

The telephone rang again.

"That will be Lisa," Farmor said. "She has called at least ten times this morning."

And it was.

"Lotte, they say your Mor—"

"It's perfectly true!" Lotte said, and she could hear how many of her friends were crowding around to hear what Lisa was finding out. Fru Fugl wanted to speak to Mor, and while they talked, Lotte sat smiling at Mor and at Farmor and at Hr. Axel and at the whole incredible world.